WHEN Cassandra descended the stairs in her new dancing dress of deep pine green trimmed in white lace, drawing on her gloves as she walked, Edward found himself unable to think further. He caught the light sweet scent of her cologne and frowned at his own feelings, puzzled. As he took his place opposite her at the long table, he noted that the candle-light softened the rosy glow of her skin until it was almost luminous, and that she had a certain trick of inclining her head ever so slightly to one side that was absolutely charming. Suddenly he found himself wondering if he was falling in love with his own wife.

If Cassie had only known this, things might have been very different that night.

THE CASSANDRA KNOT

Rebecca Baldwin

FAWCETT CREST • NEW YORK

To Blanche

THE CASSANDRA KNOT

Published by Fawcett Crest Books, a unit of CBS Publications, the Consumer Publishing Division of CBS Inc.

Copyright © 1979 by Rebecca Baldwin

ISBN: 0-449-24047-9

Selection of the Doubleday Romance Library

Printed in the United States of America

10   9   8   7   6   5   4   3   2   1

CHAPTER
1

"SO, Lady Gunneston's bringing out another one of her daughters tonight? Which one is it? The whey-faced one, or the sad one with spots? I can never keep them straight."

Edward Talbot, something less than resplendent in his evening dress, stood before the mirror over the cold fireplace, giving his thick brown hair a half-hearted shuffle of his hand, with all the appearance of a man who disliked debutante balls. Yanking uncomfortably at his stock, he turned to smile down at the elegant gentleman seated before him. "The Gunnestons are your cousins, Geoff. You should know!"

Sir Geoffrey Russell-Broome, a portrait of fashionable elegance in his well-cut evening dress, leaned back in his chair and regarded the eighth Duke of Woodland through pained eyes. "It's Selene, Edward, and she don't have spots anymore. But, I say, that waistcoat is dashed dowdy, m'boy! You ain't in the army anymore, to be dressing so plain." Almost as an afterthought, he added, "Oh, Aunt Gunneston's bringing out Cassandra Russell, too. Which you ought to know, since she's the duchess' goddaughter!" Sadly, he sat back in his chair and regarded his friend's dress once again, shaking his head.

"Cassie? Coming out?" Edward frowned and thrust his hands into his pockets. "Why, she can't be more than fifteen!"

Sir Geoffrey shook his head slightly, lest he disarrange the glory of his cravat. "Eighteen, Edward. While you were off fighting Boney, time didn't stand still. Anyway, you may trust my aunt to attempt to squeeze a groat by bringing her out with Selene! Dashed cheese-paring woman, my aunt!"

Edward laughed ruefully. "Perhaps the Gunnestons are as blown to flinders as the Talbots. Geoff, I tell you, if there were any way around this business of being a duke, I should have found it! What good is a title if all you inherit is a pile of debts and a couple of mouldering houses, everything entailed up to the hilt? It were not for m'grandmother, Geoff, I believe I should throw it all over to you and find my fortune in America."

Geoffrey rested his chin against the handle of his walking stick and looked about the rose salon of Woodland house. Definitely shabby, he thought, his gaze flickering over the worn brocade drapes and the dark spaces on the wallpaper, where there had once hung several Holbeins and at least one Reynolds in the old duke's day. Geoff sighed and took in the details of Edward's dress again. For Sir Geoffrey, who prided himself on being a top-o'-the-trees in matters of fashion, winced when he spotted a minute darn under the tails of Edward's coat. "Really, Edward, there are ways of managing to run on credit, you know. If the word went around that the Duke of Woodland patronized Scott, or Nugee, or even Weston, then there could be a very discreet arrangement about credit."

Edward's crooked smile lit up his narrow gray eyes. For the first time, Geoffrey noticed that his friend's dark hair was threaded with silver, and his eyes were tired. They were of an age, twenty-nine, Sir Geoffrey thought, but Edward looked older. His long narrow face—the Woodland countenance—betrayed age more swiftly than Sir Geoffrey's rather boyish features.

War, Sir Geoffrey thought, would do that to a man. And lord knew that Edward had been in the thick of it, from Spain to Waterloo. But still, the dandy thought, nodding to himself with approval, his friend's legs needed no padding, nor were his shoulders a challenge to his tailor's imagination. Shabby he might be, his clothes two years out of the Season and his evening pumps ever so slightly down at the heel, but, by God, he carried himself with pride.

"Thing of it is, Edward, you ought to hang out for an heiress," the baronet said thoughtfully. "Some rich cit's daughter, or one of those North Country females who come into town every season looking for a title."

Edward winced painfully. "Lord, Geoff!" he exclaimed, laughing, "Would you really have me leg-shackled? You know I'm not a marryin' man! And I couldn't marry some female for the sake of a few doubloons hanging over my head!" He crossed his hands over his chest and shook his head. "Besides, there are other considerations! M'grand-mother wouldn't have it, some massive female usurping her place and paying out her bills! Georgian she may be, but she's also damned proud."

"Not a marryin' man because you've got another interest, Edward!" Sir Geoffrey said thoughtfully. "There is at least one person who finds you appealing without resources, m'lad, and she ain't one to have charitable motives, either!"

Edward shrugged and collapsed into a chair, regarding his friend under his brows. "If you mean Lady Chantry, Geoff, better come out with it! And she is not the reason I won't marry a cit's daughter!"

"So you say, so you say," Geoff agreed swiftly. "But she ain't all the thing, either, Edward, especially for a man with as little of the ready as you! Liza Chantry's a strange un, and no mistake!"

Edward's face tightened. "Out with it, Geoff! What are you driving at?"

Sir Geoffrey made a meaningless gesture with his hands. "Mad, bad, and dangerous to know! Ain't that what Caro Lamb said about that Byron fellow? Same thing with Lady Chantry! They say she tricked the old lord into marryin' her, then poisoned him off when the fortune was safe in her hands! She came out of a gaming-house as Liza Goudge, and the on-dit is that her father was a whatcamecallit—one of those chaps who is always getting taken up for receiving stolen goods?"

"A fence," the duke replied.

"I can see what the army did for you, learning all that cant from that man of yours! A fence then, in Bear Alley, thick as molasses with every thief and footpad in town! That's what they say about Lady Chantry, Edward. She's ain't received anywhere! Not the sort of woman you'd take to Almack's with you, that's for sure!"

"Since I rarely patronize that establishment, I fail to

see what I have to worry about, dear boy." Edward's tone was even, if menacing. "Geoff, you and I have been friends these many years, since Eton, and I have never said a word against that fair Cyprian who took you for a phaeton and a set of matched grays with which to tool through the park!"

"Past history, dear boy! Thing is, I learned from my mistakes in the muslin company. And I would never dangle after widows as dangerous as Lady Chantry! There's something about her that looks as if she'd cut you to ribbands if you weren't careful. What's more, she must be ten years older than you! Bad ton, dear boy!"

Having said his piece, Sir Geoffrey withdrew a porcelain snuffbox from an interior pocket and took a generous pinch. "The woman's a walking scandal!"

"Perhaps," Edward said quietly. "But then, I have never had a taste for frail maidens with no experience of the world, and less for what or what is not ton. England in peacetime is a dashed bore, Geoff! And even more of a dashed bore, if all there is to worry about is an endless stream of debts and ducal obligations! I do not care for what the world may say of me!" An impish smile momentarily lightened his features. "Besides, I'm a Woodland! And we have never cared what scandals are attached to our name, as well you know, coz!"

Sir Geoffrey shook his head. "A word to the wise, Edward! Besides, I have no desire to succeed to your title if it means inheriting the old man's debts as well! Even my purse would be strained by that!"

"What, Edward, are you plotting to go to America again?"

A sturdy dowager had entered the room, drawing on her long gloves as she crossed the floor. Her round face was framed by a turban of dove silk bearing several plumes, and her ball dress of pearl-gray silk, over a slip of smoked lace, rustled as she allowed her cheek to be kissed by Sir Geoffrey, who had risen at her entrance. Upon her bosom, a large ruby set with several smaller diamonds glittered like an evil eye as she settled herself on the sofa, her sharp eyes taking in every detail of the scene with amused grace.

Playfully, she rapped at Sir Geoffrey's shoulder with the sticks of her fan, her expression alight with mischief that only dowager duchesses of a certain age may acknowledge.

"I do hope you were discussing your great-aunt Augusta, dear Geoffrey, for I believe that everyone must think I have thrust my spoon into the wall by now! It has been so long since I have appeared in Society!"

"Nonsense, dear ma'am!" Sir Geoffrey answered gallantly. "Everyone knows that you've been in mourning for the duke! Anyway, if you were dead, would Lady Gunneston invite you to her ball?"

The Dowager nodded. "Amelia Gunneston would not dare to exclude me!" Her plumes shook vigorously. "Not when my dear Cassandra is making her debut tonight! I would have risen from my bed of pain to attend this occasion. How Thomasia could have died and left the guardianship of that poor child to such a tartar as Amelia Gunneston, *I* shall never know! But she may be sure that I shall be there to make sure that everything is done properly for dear Cassandra! Poor dear child, to be cast orphaned into that vampire's nest—or do I mean viper's nest?" She tapped her fan against her cheek in a manner that did not bode well for any possible mistakes Lady Gunneston might make as a hostess.

"Poor Cassandra, my foot! Your pardon, ma'am," Sir Geoffrey said, flicking an invisible speck of lint from his collar. "Why, when she marries, she'll be one of the richest women in England! She inherits every penny of old Golden Ball Russell's fortune! After tonight, the girl won't be safe from the bucks!"

"And I wish well to the man who catches her!" Edward added. "There was never such a girl to be into scrapes! You remember, Geoff, when we were down from school, the night she persuaded me to dress up in a sheet and frighten the governess half to death, believing the Gunneston ghost was walking again?"

"Cassandra is a very lively girl!" the Dowager laughed.

Sir Geoffrey bowed in her direction. "Just the sort of thing m'grandfather was likely to say that you and he would do in your younger days, m'am! But the rare scene Aunt Gunneston kicked up about that one! You'd think we'd all committed murder and robbery!" He shook his head, grimacing. "She kicked up a rare fuss and no mistake! Never saw such a dragon of a woman in my life as my Aunt Gunneston. Sallow-faced and evil-tempered, always acting as if Cassie were there on charity, instead of the very good allowance the trustees paid out to her year after year for the girl's upkeep! Sent Devon through Oxford on that money, they did, at least until he was sent down the last time."

"What? Dishonourable Devon at Oxford?" Edward exclaimed. "What a cram they must have had to get him in!"

The Dowager was not interested in the exploits of the Gunneston heir. Brushing him aside with a fan-wave, she concentrated on his mother. "Amelia Gunneston was always an excessively grasping female! I have never liked her—indeed, I have always detested her, for there is not a spark of kindness in her soul, for all of her pious ravings about her Christian duty! My heart has always gone out to poor Cassandra. Her mother and I were very close. If our circumstances had been different, I should have taken the child into my house. A duke must always take precedence over a baron, after all."

"Wouldn't have worked out anyway, Grand'mère," Edward reminded her. "We could barely keep home and hearth together as it was." He shifted uncomfortably. "As a matter of fact, Peeksell came around this morning, with an offer for the house—a very generous offer. It would settle all our debts if we sold this pile and moved up to Woodland Manor."

The Dowager sighed. "I doubt that anything could pay off a large part of our debts, let alone the whole amount. They seem endless."

Sir Geoffrey tactfully examined his snuffbox. Although he was quite aware of the state of the Woodland affairs, he preferred not be drawn into a family discussion of the problem.

"If I could sell off the title, I think I would do it. There, at least, the Italians have the right idea! It's been nothing but trouble to any of us!"

"If your grandfather could have done so, I believe he would have." The Dowager sighed. "He sold off everything else! Such a charming man, but sadly addicted to gambling. We are fortunate that my dowry and your mother's dowry were the only things he could not touch!"

Edward nodded fondly at the old woman, amused and exasperated by her Georgian frankness. "I suppose you are right. But sometimes I think it was rather inconsiderate of my parents to go off to Italy and drown in Lake Como, leaving you to raise a schoolboy alone! I never wanted to be a duke!"

"Very good thing, being a duke," Sir Geoffrey said absently. "Wouldn't mind being a duke, if it weren't for the debts. And of course, I don't wish you dead, Edward, not at all!"

"I should hope not, dear Geoff! I can't see you spending a year in black for me!" Edward laughed and drew out his watch. "The time grows later. I suggest we make our appearance at Lady Gunneston's and leave as early as possible. I swore, after the duke was finished with us at Waterloo, that I would never attend another ball as long as I lived!"

From the ballroom of Lady Gunneston's house on Upper Mount Street, the soft strains of a country dance drifted through the air. Lady Gunneston did not approve of the waltz, even if it had been sanctioned by Almack's.

Lady Gunneston herself, a hatchet-faced woman in a severe puce gown, stood ready to receive her guests at the head of the stairs. Beside her stood two young females, both attired in demure, debutante pastels.

The taller one was clearly her mother's daughter. Although she possessed a head of lustrous black curls, and her slender figure was set off to advantage by her gown of palest pink, it was all too patent that she bade fair to resemble her mother in both face and temperament. The taller girl seemed by comparison to be a mouse.

Although she was eighteen and in the first blush of her youth, it was clear that Cassandra Russell was no diamond of the first water. Her skin was rosy, rather than fashionably pale, and her wheat-colored hair displayed too much of a mind of its own to be contained by the severe, virginal bands demanded of young ladies. Her face was heart-shaped and rather piquant, sadly lacking in the classic planing of her cousin's face. Her nose was too short and her eyes too large and too green. And, as the Woodland party came up the stairs, her mouth was turned down at the corners in a most unhappy manner, as if she wished herself a thousand miles away.

The pale lavender gown she wore was neither cut to show off her figure to advantage, nor to flatter her complexion. Almost defiantly, she had woven a circlet of white roses through her hair and fastened a seed-pearl band about her neck.

At least part of her discomfort was evidently caused by the presence of a spotty youth in a loud waistcoat hovering close to her shoulder, squeezing her reluctant hand between his own as he whispered in her ear. Despite her obvious embarrassment at this situation, her Aunt Gunneston smiled upon this situation with approval.

"Amelia!" the Dowager said grandly, presenting her hand to her old rival, drawing herself up to her full imposing height while she leveled the spotty youth with one quelling glance and a slightly raised brow.

"Dear Augusta!" Lady Gunneston exuded through clenched teeth, gesturing the young man away with her fan. She sketched the slightest of curtseys for the Dowager. "May I present my daughter Selene Louisa, and my niece, Cassandra Mary Russell?"

"We are acquainted," the duchess said coldly, giving the hapless Selene the slightest nod and moving immediately to clasp Cassandra's shoulders. "Dear child!" she murmured in tones used for martyrs of the utmost suffering.

Leaving Edward and Geoffrey to exchange uncomfortable glances, she immediately launched into a low-voiced conversation with her godchild.

"Dragon at the gates!" Sir Geoffrey muttered. "Told you so!"

Lady Gunneston's stiff smile fixed on Edward, and she grasped his hand in her own. "Dear Duke! How gracious of you to honor us! You know, of course, my daughter Selene, and my niece, Cassandra—"

Selene dropped a curtsey, giggling. "Edward," she gasped, in a waterfall of giggles that made Edward wince. He bowed over her hand and turned to Cassandra.

Miss Russell, still clutching the Dowager's hand, met Edward's look with startled green eyes. For a second, Edward wondered if there was pleading in those green eyes, but the thought was quickly put away. Certainly, he thought, the Dowager's goddaughter had grown up and let down her skirts, but the ugly duckling had not changed into a swan, and in fact, looked uncomfortable.

Already he felt the boredom stealing over him, wishing he were at Jackson's, or his club, or anywhere but another dashed stuffy ball full of simpering, marriage-minded misses.

Selene had claimed his attention, chattering on in a mindless fashion interrupted by a chorus of giggles at whatever inanities he chose to mutter. He talked to her with only half his mind, already calculating the time it would take to circulate once through the room and leave the Dowager in the capable hands of Sir Geoffrey.

The spotty youth, dancing attendance in the background, caught his eye, and Edward exclaimed aloud: "Dishonourable Devon! How long have you been on the town?"

Devonshire Gunneston, now a baron, glanced up in some surprise, and an unattractive blush suffused his face.

Rather ineffectually, he raised a quizzing glass to his eye and surveyed Edward through the lens. "I say, Woodland!" he exclaimed.

"Dear Cousin Selene!" Sir Geoffrey murmured, rather too pointedly, at Edward's elbow, giving his friend a slight nudge. "That's a dashed fetching gown. Madame Celeste or Mrs. Handley?"

Miss Gunneston, aware of Sir Geoffrey's reputation as a man of fashion, once again turned on the waterfall, and Edward made his escape.

"Cassie," he said simply, taking her hand. The green eyes flashed at him. "You've grown up, my girl."

Cassandra nodded. "I'm eighteen, Edward. And you've returned to us as quite a hero. We've read all about your bravery on the Peninsula, and at Waterloo." As their hands touched, Edward felt a slip of paper being pressed into his palm. Without missing a beat, she continued, "It is so very good to see you again."

Edward betrayed nothing as his hand went to the

pocket of his waistcoat, and his hand emerged empty. "You flatter me, Cassie."

"She keeps all the newspaper clippings in her missal," Devon brayed loudly.

Cassandra flushed slightly and turned away. Devon, Edward guessed, was foxed already. His protuberant eyes and slack mouth were moist, and his breath reeked of brandy.

"I say, Woodland, there's talk of you going up against the great Jackson himself on Tuesday next! Quite the Corinthian!"

Edward permitted himself the thinnest smile. Generations of ducal breeding seemed to rise up in him as he stared through Devon's face with frightening hauteur. "Boxing cant is hardly suitable conversation at a ball, Dev!" he said thinly, bowing over Cassandra's hand. "Servant, Cassie! Trust I may have the honor of dancing with you later, if your card is not filled up yet?"

"I have a boulanger open," Cassandra said. Her green eyes were grateful. Swiftly Edward scribbled his name across her dance program. "Grand'mère, I see Lady Ombersley signaling you across the room."

The Dowager's plumes nodded. "I will only be in town for a short time, my dear, but I hope that you will pay a call in Grosvenor Square before I return to Woodland Manor, my love!"

"Of course, ma'am." Cassandra replied, taking hold of the old lady's hand and clutching at it a moment longer than necessary.

Fear, Edward thought, and was surprised. He had never known Cassandra Russell to be afraid of anything, but there seemed to be a flea in her ear tonight.

Edward escorted his grandmother to the Dowagers' corner, making sure that she was served a glass of arrack, that her shawls and fan were situated well within her reach, and that Lady Ombersley was as well as ever. Then he excused himself and disappeared among the dancers.

Finding a secluded alcove, he dipped into his waistcoat pocket and produced the scrap of paper Cassandra had pressed into his hand. Unfolding it, he read:

EDWARD—I AM IN DESPERATE TROUBLE AND ONLY YOU CAN HELP ME. PLEASE MEET ME IN THE CONSERVATORY AT ELEVEN-FIFTEEN. DO NOT FAIL ME NOW. EVER, C.

The duke read this curious message through twice. The second time, the ducal eyebrows rose, and a slight, sardonic smile twisted his face. Tucking the scrap of paper into his pocket, he drifted out into the floor again. Either Cassie had gotten herself into another one of her scrapes again, or he would arrive in the conservatory at the appointed hour to find the housemaids lined up singing "Hasten Unto the World." With Lady Cassandra Russell, anything was possible, he thought, his eyes surveying the crowded ballroom. Perhaps tonight would not be as dull as he had supposed.

"Edward! We have not seen you at Almack's since your return!" With a slight start, the duke turned to find his old friend Lady Jersey at his elbow, her delicate frame becomingly gowned in sea-green silk. Playfully, she rapped at his wrist with her fan, continuing on in her, breathy voice, "I have just spoken to the duchess, who told me you were here. I could scarce believe it, since we never see you anywhere anymore. But how enchanting your grandmamma looks! She says she only comes to town once in a very great while now, and still, she knows all the latest on-dits!" The Lady's bubbling laugh was infectious, for Edward found himself chuckling. "Only fancy, such a sad crush here tonight. The Gunneston girl is taking enough, but one must feel that Lady Cassandra Russell is not a great beauty. It is a good thing she has a large fortune and a winning personality. Of course, the way her aunt dresses her—" Lady Jersey shook her head sadly.

"Well, Sally, I see that I find you as full of spirits as ever," Edward remarked. "If all the patronesses were as charming as you, perhaps I would appear at Almack's more often."

"You will bring Her Grace one evening, I hope? She is so anxious to see Lady Cassandra enjoy her first Season." Lady Jersey's eyes sparkled. "Of course, from what one hears, dear Edward, debutantes seem to bore you."

There was mischief in her eye as she spoke these words and Edward shook his head. Signaling a passing waiter, he procured two glasses of champagne. "So, Sally, m'grandmother's been talking to you. Pray, what did she say?"

Lady Jersey sifted the fringes of her silk shawl through her fingers. "That Lady Cassandra's debut was not the only reason she had made the journey from Devonshire in this cold weather." She sipped at her champagne demurely. "It seems that she is concerned about you, Edward."

The duke groaned. "I should have known. Dash it, Sal, you know I'm deuced fond of my grandmother, but one never knows what she will do next, or say next! And of course, she would never tell me directly what's troubling her. Lady Chantry, I suppose?"

Lady Jersey nodded. "Apparently rumors of your— attachment—have reached her in Devonshire." Lady Jersey shook her head. "Bad ton, Edward, excessively bad ton!" She laughed and rolled her eyes. "But seriously, my friend, your relationship with Lady Chantry *is* one of the on-dits of town, and I think it has your grandmother more worried than she would care to admit, or she would not have confided in *me*."

The duke nodded. "I understand, Sally, and I thank you for your discretion."

She bowed slightly, her eyes serious. "It is not my business to speak of such things, you know, but your grandmother has been one of my friends since I came out, and I felt that I ought to speak to you." She gestured helplessly with her fan.

"I assure you, it is the most cynical of relationships in this most cynical of ages," Edward said drily. "Neither of us demands anything from the other except companionship." He glanced around the room at the glittering throng. "I daresay half the ladies here have indulged in conduct more scandalous than Lady Chantry's."

Lady Jersey sipped her champagne again. "Oh quite, but *they* are discreet, Edward." She laid a hand against his arm, forcing him to meet her eyes. "And Edward, you must be discreet, also, for her sake. I think she is pained that you have not settled down with a nice female and given her grandchildren. As one gets older, one thinks of those things."

"In time, Sal, in time," Edward promised. "And now, if you would do me the honor of dancing with me, I believe that I will not tromp on your slippers, rough soldier that I am!"

"War," sighed Lady Jersey, "has done terrible things to you, Edward. You've changed so much. Once you were gentle and oh, more idealistic than you are now."

"And what am I now, Sally?" the duke asked, stepping through the quadrille with his lively partner.

The patroness shook her head. "Oh, hardened, somehow. Cynical, as you say, and—" Her eyes narrowed. "Dangerous. I feel as if you might be capable of anything now, Edward. And it is not just you. It's all the young men who marched off to war and came back disillusioned and cynical, as if they'd been through Hell."

Edward's gray eyes were cold as steel under his lids. "Perhaps we have been through Hell, Sally," he said lightly. "That's what makes Liza so—attractive to me. We're both survivors, I think, in our own ways. She demands nothing of me but an understanding of—shall we say, our mutual boredom with polite society?"

Lady Jersey smiled, but for once, Silence was silent.

Cassandra, sitting in a Burma chair half-hidden by palm trees, twisted her long gloves nervously through her fingers. From time to time, she glanced up at the open door of the conservatory, as if afraid of discovery. One slippered foot tapped impatiently at the gravel floor. She closed her eyes. "Please, Edward," she said under her breath, "please come."

Even on a cold November evening, the conservatory was stiflingly hot. From above her head, tiny droplets of water fell from an orchid basket into her hair, sparkling like diamonds among the errant curls.

This situation was not exactly what she had pictured, crouching like a housemaid. But it was the only way she could think of to see Edward alone.

Aunt Amelia's ever-watchful eye was swift to note and punish Cassandra for the smallest transgression of the older woman's many rules. Even in a household more joyful than the Gunneston establishment, a young lady could not meet a gentleman alone, even for a few minues. But Cassandra had learned over the years how to circumvent her aunt.

She was rubbing her nose with the tip of her glove when he came in the doorway, looking about the room, his mouth twisted with amusement.

"Hsst!" Cassandra whispered, her heart thundering in her ears, "Edward!" She gestured at him frantically.

Touching his cravat, Edward frowned at his childhood friend. "Cassie, what the devil does this mean?" He waved the note under her nose. "Very improper of you to be passing notes at your own debut!"

Cassandra took the note from his fingers and shredded it into the dirt of the palm. "You know it would be impossible for me to see you any other way, Edward! Aunt keeps an eye on all of us, and if she's not there, you may depend upon Selene's carrying the tale. You have no idea what it's like to live this way! I feel as if I'm in a convent! I'm not allowed to go out, nor see people, or—anything that I would like to do!"

Blushing furiously, she looked down at her feet. Slowly she focused her gaze on his face, looking at him under her lashes. "Edward, I'm in very serious trouble! You would not believe what a tangle things are in!"

The duke's face betrayed a slow smile. He shook his head. "Cassie, in all the years I have known you, you have been nothing but trouble! And no, I will not put a bucket of water over the governess' door, nor will I dress up in a sheet and climb in the transom to scare the footmen!"

Cassandra shook her head, annoyed. "Edward, it is not that at all! When I let down my skirts and did up my hair, I put all that foolishness behind me. This is much more serious, Edward. I—" She took a deep breath and closed her eyes. "I have a proposition for you!"

For the first time in six years, Edward Talbot took a good look at Cassandra Russell. She had, he admitted to himself, grown up. True, she was no beauty, but she was passable. With the right clothes, and a change of hairstyle, she would even be quite attractive, he thought. It was just the sort of project that someone like Geoffrey would enjoy.

As if she had read his thoughts, Cassandra smoothed down the skirt of her gown. "It is hideous, isn't it? Believe me, I did not choose the color. You may depend upon Aunt Amelia for that! She wanted to make sure that I would look as unattractive as possible tonight, lest I should attract a suitor!"

Edward said nothing. Cassandra looked down at her feet, still twisting her gloves. "I daresay you think I'm exaggerating, but I'm not! I am allowed to attend only the most select parties, which means that all the people there are the Gunnestons' friends, and Selene is to go to Almack's while I am not! Aunt Amelia means for me to marry Devon!" she announced in tones of total loathing.

"What?" Edward exclaimed.

Cassandra nodded miserably. "So, therefore, I am not allowed to do *anything,* lest I should be cast in the way of someone I might form a *tendre* for!"

From an interior pocket, Edward withdrew a silver case and extracted a cigarillo. Frowning, he lit up, exhaling a cloud of blue smoke. Was this a jest, he wondered. Looking at her tight and pale face, he knew it was not.

"I am to feel grateful, you see, that Aunt Amelia took me in when I was an orphan. Our engagement is to be announced in the *Post* shortly." Cassandra shuddered. "She told me yesterday, in that terrible way she has, that it had all been decided."

"Why didn't you say no?" Edward asked reasonably. "If someone told me I was to marry Dishonourable Devon, I should say no."

"You could! I could not! The—persuasions she would use are not pleasant! You don't understand what a dragon Aunt Amelia can be when she has her mind set on something! She is so threatening and so unpleasant that I shake in my shoes, Edward. But I would rather be dead than married to Devon!"

Edward, who knew quite a bit more about young Gunneston's career on the town than he cared to admit to Cassandra, understood perfectly. "So," he said quietly, "she wishes to keep the fortune in the family, hey? And how long will it take Devon to run through your money? A year? Two years?"

Cassandra shook her head. "He is awful. He always has been awful. You don't know how many of the house-maids have left because of him! Yet to Aunt Amelia, he can do no wrong! To her, it is the greatest honor imaginable that I should marry Devon!" She laughed bitterly. "I'd sooner drown myself in the Serpentine, Edward, I swear I should!"

"What about your trustees?" Edward asked.

"Oh, whatever Aunt Amelia thinks is fine with them. Old Spreckles is completely under her thumb! They don't care about me at all! And it has been so terrible here! Aunt is so tight-fisted! Tallow candles and turned-down dresses, and we are not allowed fires in our rooms, even in the coldest winter! Do you wonder why all my cousins have married rich men? They were sold off like cattle to the highest bidder! But I could have endured it, if I knew that I would have a Season, but even that is to be taken away from me! Since I am to marry Devon, Aunt sees no use in my going out, or attending anything but the most stuffy family parties! And, if I do not marry Devon, Aunt is threatening to lock me in my room until I see the light." Cassandra shuddered unhappily. A large tear formed in the corner of her eye and rolled down her cheek.

Edward wrapped himself in a cloud of smoke. Only someone who knew the Gunneston family as well as he did could picture the tyrannies exacted by Lady Gunneston. A cold anger filled his heart and he clenched his fists. "I cannot believe that Spreckles could countenance such a move. Surely, if you were to complain to him—"

Cassandra shrugged. "Oh, no! He is delighted that the

money will be kept in the family, you see. And I do have a great deal of money," she added naïvely.

Suddenly she looked up. "Edward," she said softly, putting her hand on his arm and looking up at him through moist eyes. "Are you as far up the River Tick as everyone says?"

The duke's cigarillo dropped from his fingers and fell to the gravel. For a moment, Cassandra thought he would strike her, but his face dissolved into a laugh. "Oh, lord, Cass, where did you learn that phrase?"

"Devon," she replied. "But the point is, are you in debt, Edward? Everyone says that you are as poor as a pikestaff, that the duchess' husband gambled everything away, and lost what was left in the Waterloo Panic, before he died."

Edward nodded. "Yes, Cassie," he said slowly, "it's all true. I've never made any pretense that it wasn't. The old guv died under a pile of debts. Everything's been sold except the houses and some of my grandmother's jewels, the ones that were entailed with the estate. If I'd known what trouble it was to be a duke, I should never have sold out my commission!"

Cassandra dabbed at her eyes with her glove. "It's true, then? It's terribly bad?"

"Almost hopeless," Edward said. "Not at all like the dukes you read about in fairy tales, Cassie! Grandmamma and I are as poor as church mice. I had to promise my man half his salary this week so he'd get me ready to come to your aunt's ball!"

Cassandra bit her lip. "I would rather be dead than marry Devon, with his wet mouth and his pop eyes! So, you see, I thought and thought, and there was no one I really liked very much, except of course, Geoffrey, but Geoffrey had said so many times he wasn't a marrying man, and I thought about you, and all the problems you were having with money, and I've known you forever and ever, and we've always gotten on very well, and I thought, you know, that perhaps we could be a way out of one another's problems."

"Cassandra," Edward said terribly, "are you suggesting that I *marry* you?"

"Yes," Cassandra said miserably, with a flood of tears. She was not, Edward reflected, a female who looked well in tears. "It's the only way out, you see," she whispered, twisting her fingers through the gloves in her lap.

"What?" Edward repeated, stunned.

"It's the only way out, Edward. Aunt cannot possibly refuse to countenance an offer from a duke. Even Spreckles would question such an action, even if the duke were you, and you don't have a feather to fly with! And I should try to make you a good wife. I wouldn't interfere with your other attachments, or keep you under the cat's foot, or question your spending. And of course, you would have a large part of my money to pay off your debts and set up your estates again. It would be a marriage of convenience, you see."

Edward Talbot sat back in his chair, stunned. "Cassandra," he said in a choked voice, "are you bamboozling me?"

She looked up at him. Her eyes were red-rimmed. "No, Edward, I am not. I've never been more serious in my life," she said meekly.

Stung by unaccustomed sympathy, Edward reached out and took her hand. "Cassie, I'm very flattered that you asked me, but it's out of the question. I could only hurt you, damage your fortune, and set you up as a laughing-stock in the eyes of the world. Marrying you for your money, Cass? That would be out of the question."

Several more tears rolled down her cheeks. "I'm sorry," she said in a small choked voice. "But, Edward, you have no idea how very hard it is to face the idea of marriage to Devon. I'll drown myself in the Serpentine first, I really will!"

Her voice was so fierce that Edward started. Cassandra's chin was thrust forward, and her mouth was tight. "If you only understood how very unhappy I am! If I were a married lady, and a duchess, I could do just as I pleased, and no one would be telling me that I was ugly or stupid, or—had to marry Devon Gunneston!" She burst into a full torrent of racking sobs, burying her face in her hands.

Edward's mouth set firmly. Gently, he lifted Cassandra's face to his own. "Is it really so terrible then, Cass?" he asked gently.

She nodded. "And if we were married, you would have money, and you could buy all sorts of things. You could let the duchess go to Bath twice a year, just as she would like, and you could do all sorts of things! And it would be so nice to be related to the duchess! She is so kind to me, you know!" Cassandra bit her lip. "And you could buy Lady Chantry some jewelry, too!"

Mention of his grandmother and his mistress in the same breath made Edward want to laugh. "How do you know about Lady Chantry? Don't you know that well-brought-up females do not mention gentlemen's liaisons?"

Cassandra shook her head miserably. "I am ugly and stupid and I have no tact! Oh, Edward, I am so sorry, but everyone knows anyway, so what difference does it make?"

Edward could only shake his head helplessly. "Cass, you are mad!"

"We could each go our own way. I daresay Woodland House is large enough that we could wander about in it for days and never see one another," Cassandra said wistfully.

Edward sighed, reaching out to touch her wheat-colored hair. It felt rough and coarse, not at all like Liza's smooth, silky, raven tresses. Cassandra was not at all like Elizabeth Chantry, he thought absurdly, as if it mattered. A vision of his mistress flashed before his eyes. Elizabeth, with her violet eyes and coal-black hair, laughing as she sipped at her champagne, the jewels about her white throat reflected in the crystal glass. He wondered what Elizabeth would say when she heard of his engagement. She would laugh, would say that she wished him well of his new bride, as her white arms drew him down into her soft bed. She'd wish him well of his heiress bride.

Little Cassandra, he thought, so like a child. Gently, he stroked her hair. A frown creased his brow. He had always rather liked Cassandra; she was pluck to the backbone when they were children; there was nothing that she would not try. But what was she now? A rather colorless female in a badly chosen lavender gown. Her silk slippers were scuffed, and she was wiping her nose on her gloves. Aside from Elizabeth, there was no other woman in his life, and he did not love Elizabeth. War and blood and fear had driven the emotion of love away from him, Edward thought sadly. But why not? Cassandra was good-natured and pliable. Naïve she might be, but she was never dull. Perhaps it was time that he settled down, provided his grandmother with a great-grandchild. And the Dowager would be pleased with his choice of bride. Cassandra would never have been his choice, of course. He liked his women older and more voluptuous.

Looking down at her heaving shoulders, Edward thought of Lady Gunneston's gray, greedy face. For a second, he understood the terror she could inspire in Cassandra; it must be like Boney's cannons. And the thought of Devon Gunneston's conduct, in a certain discreet establishment patronized by gentlemen of the ton, made Edward shudder for Cassandra. No, he could not allow that. Cassandra would make a good duchess, he knew, for she would do her duty and conduct herself with propriety as she had been trained from childhood.

And, he damned himself, there was the money to be thought of. It would be a good arrangement. Cassandra expected nothing of him, after all, nor he of her—

"Cassandra Russell, will you do me the honor of becoming my bride?" Edward asked her softly.

Cassandra turned up her tear-streaked face. Her smile was the sun coming out from behind a cloud. She grasped Edward's hand in hers. "Are you sure? I didn't mean to cry about it, really I didn't, Edward. I'm not a crybaby. You know that."

"Indeed, you are not, Cassie," he said softly, putting

his arm about her shoulders. "You are as pluck to the backbone as they come, and somehow or other we'll get through."

She wiped at her eyes. "Really, Edward?" she asked. "I promise, I will not be the least bit of trouble to you, or cause you any grief about—about the other thing."

"Let me worry about that," Edward said formally, standing up. "I shall call on your aunt tomorrow, and we shall be married as soon as the banns are posted. There is no reason for either of us to wait." He smiled. "We'd better go back. It seems to me that you promised me a dance. And I would like to tell Grand'mère the news."

CHAPTER
2

IN the cold north light of the breakfast parlor, Edward stared down balefully at his egg. He pushed the plate across the cloth and stirred his tea. "I must have been mad. It must be one of Cassie's little knots. I mean, dash it, you cannot force a female into marriage against her will. The idea went out with the Tudors. She's been reading too many Gothic novels."

The Dowager, doing full justice to a trencher loaded with eggs, bacon, kidneys, muffins and jam, to be washed down with a pot of strong black coffee, smiled indulgently upon her grandson's anxiety over his engagement. "Foolishness, my love, is not in Cassandra's nature. And if you knew the number of females I could number among our own friends who have been more or less forced into marriages distasteful to them, you would believe that it can and does happen every day. You don't think the Gunning sisters married for love, do you? Once you are quite used to the idea of engagement and marriage, it will not seem to be so harsh. Your papa was quite in a snit for weeks, but at last, both times, he came about. And was glad." The Dowager selected another muffin and began to cover it generously with jam. "Cassandra is a trifle high-spirited at times, but I daresay that comes of living under the cat's paw in Amelia's household. Once she is properly established as a duchess, I do not see why she will not conduct herself as decorously as—well, as I do."

Edward glared at his grandmother's frilled morning cap, bent over her plate. He wanted very much to ask her why she could not stay abed until noon like most of her contemporaries, but thought better of it. But, as one of the two *partis* to this unholy alliance between himself and Cassandra, she was being remarkably unsympathetic this morning. Then, of course, Cassandra was her goddaughter, and she must be gloating about this latest triumph over Amelia Gunneston. Edward sipped at his tea thoughtfully. Sir Geoffrey, the other *parti,* he realized, would be equally unsympathetic to any clear, rational thought on the matter. Again, he sighed.

"And indeed, dear Edward, I do think it was time you were thinking of setting up your nursery. Much as I love

Geoffrey, I simply do not feel that he is proper ducal material. He lacks a certain training for the role, the responsibilities, don't you know." The Dowager beamed upon her grandson fondly. "In my delicate health, when I may be carried off at any time, it would be such a comfort to know that my grandchildren's children would remember me." She helped herself to another small forkful of kidney and smiled beatifically upon her grandson. "Edward, you could do far worse than marry Cassandra. Even if she were not already practically one of the family, her birth and her lineage are quite acceptable. I believe she is one hundred and thirty-seventh in line for the throne, whereas you are only one hundred and fifty-ninth, and Devon Gunneston would wade barefoot through her fortune before you could sneeze. Since Cassandra has been in and out of Woodland House and Woodland Manor all her life, it would simply be a way of more firmly attaching her to us. But if she had not a penny to her name and came to the door in her petticoat, I should still welcome her as your wife."

"A pretty speech, ma'am." Edward said drily. "But you do not have to beard the dragon in her lair."

The Dowager sat up. Her eyes twinkled. "I could accompany you—" she began, but Edward had thrown down his napkin and left the table.

The Dowager looked at his retreating back and shook her head slightly. When she was certain he was out of earshot, she smiled. "And I would give anything I own to see Amelia Gunneston's face when you ask for her niece's hand in marriage," she murmured softly. Quite content, she rang for another pot of coffee, and made a mental note to send for Sir Geoffrey to call upon her as soon as

he awoke. As Sir Geoffrey did not stir from his slumbers
until eleven or so, that gave her at least three full hours.
"A marriage is announced between Lady Cassandra Mary
Russell and His Grace, Edward Talbot, Eighth Duke of
Woodland, Baron Hyne and Edgworth," she composed
aloud. "That should do very well for the *Post*. Yes, Far-
rell, I should like another pot of coffee, if you please,"
she told the footman. "And I should like it served in
the writing room."

Grandly, the Dowager rose from the table, already
planning the day's activities. But, thinking again of Lady
Gunneston, she chuckled.

After rendering up his card to Jackson, Lady Gunneston's long-suffering butler, Edward found himself
ushered into the drawing room to wait her ladyship's
pleasure. Nervously, he tugged at his cravat and thumbed
through a back issue of *La Belle Assemblée,* still unable
to believe that he was actually going through with this
charade. Torn between a print of a truly hideous *costume
de bal* and the need to come to grips with the reality of
the situation, he was startled by a scratching sound at
the door.

Lady Cassandra Russell herself, attired in an unflatter-
ing gown of magenta merino, her hair untidily piled on
top of her head and bound back with a dingy bit of ribband, hovered uncertainly under the threshold. "Edward!
Thank God you came! Jackson came immediately to tell
me, before he went up to Aunt Amelia. He is convinced,
you know, that ours is the grand romance of the Season!"
She drew her hand across the bridge of her nose, leaving
a wide blue streak of watercolor on her skin.

Edward, seeing his future bride thus attired and decorated, again doubted his sanity in entering into this bargain, but he smiled and rose politely. "I said I would, didn't I, Cassie? Damn, what do you think I am? I gave my word—"

Cassie frantically motioned him to be quiet. "She'll hear us, and then, oh there will be hell to pay, Edward. Listen, you must tell her that ours has been a long-standing secret attachment, that you did not wish to speak to her until I had made my come-out, but now that your mourning period is over, and I have made my debut, there can be no further question of our marriage. It's the only thing she will believe, Edward."

The duke raised one brow, but said nothing. Cassandra leaned in the doorway, childlike and wide-eyed. "Edward, I am so grateful. I promise I won't make a fuss, or disgrace you, or do any of those things that I am not supposed to do. I—"

"There, Lady Cassie," Jackson said in conspiratorial tones as he appeared around her shoulder. "She's expecting His Grace upstairs, so do you run back to the young ladies' room before she catches you here, and change your dress, miss, for I've no doubt she'll be sending for you right enough." As Cassandra disappeared, Jackson's face assumed its bland mask. "If you please, Your Grace, Lady Gunneston will receive you now," he said professionally.

Edward followed the butler up the stairs to Lady Gunneston's salon. Just before the man opened the door to announce the duke, he turned and smiled. "If Your Grace will permit, sir, having known you and Lady Cassie both since you were in leading strings—well, we are behind you to a man, Your Grace."

"Thanks, Jackson," Edward said drily. "And Her Ladyship?"

"Is completely in ignorance of these happy events, sir."

Duke and butler exchanged a look of complete understanding. Jackson opened the door. "His Grace, the Duke of Woodland, my lady," he announced smoothly, and stepped back to allow Edward into the dragon's lair.

Lady Gunneston was seated at her writing desk, attired in a bleak-looking morning dress. As Edward entered the room, she rose from her chair and extended a thin, cold hand to him. "Dear Edward, please come in. I hope you will forgive the disorder, but we are still at sixes and sevens from last night's ball. Dear Devon was—taken rather ill in the course of the evening, I fear, and—" She shrugged, indicating a chair near the low fire. "Boys will be boys, after all."

The duke seated himself uneasily, watching Lady Gunneston's thin back as she straightened the papers on the desk and seated herself opposite him. The smile she gave him was cold and did not quite reach her eyes. "Now, Edward, what may I do for you?" she asked, adjusting a shawl about her thin shoulders. "Jackson gives me to believe you have called on some personal matter involving the Gunnestons. Naturally, we had hoped for the best for Selene. Her fortune is adequate, and she may look as high as she pleases, but I had hoped to have her out for a while before entertaining any proposals."

Studying Edward's expression for half a second, she

frowned. "If you've come about any of Devon's debts, I'm afraid you'll have to settle that with him. I have no money, not a farthing to spend on his gaming debts."

"I have come about neither Selene or Devon, ma'am," Edward said crisply "although I wish you well of both of them. Actually, I have come to discuss the matter of Cassandra." Much to his own surprise, Edward found himself enjoying this duel. Confronting Lady Gunneston not as a schoolboy but as a duke was a most enjoyable change.

Lady Gunneston's jaw dropped slightly, and her hand clenched around the arm of her chair. "Cassandra? What has she done now? If she's played another one of her hoydenish pranks, I am very much afraid that I shall have to punish her very severely." The faintest trace of pleasure appeared, unbeckoned, about Lady Gunneston's eyes, and Edward suddenly understood Cassandra's terror of the woman, and knew that those stories about Devon were not unfounded. Anger pricked at him, and he drew himself up to his full height, every inch the military man, every inch the duke.

"Cassandra has done nothing, I assure you. At least nothing to be ashamed of. The fact is, Lady Gunneston, I have come to ask your permission to marry Cassandra Russell."

A slow, feline smile tensed at the corners of Lady Gunneston's mouth. It was unpleasant. But Edward reminded himself that he was no schoolboy, and faced her down squarely with a look that had sent the men under his command running. Lady Gunneston retreated a fraction of an inch into her chair, but the smile did not leave her lips. "I am afraid that is impossible, Your Grace," Lady Gunneston said smoothly.

Edward raised one brow. "And may I ask why?"

"Because, Edward, Cassandra is engaged to marry Devon," Lady Gunneston said triumphantly. She inclined her head, watching Edward's face.

He did not move. "I fail to see how Cassandra and Devon could be engaged when I have been secretly engaged to her for four years. We plighted our troth before I left for Spain. At the time, of course, I felt she was too young to marry, and many things may happen to a man in wartime. But I have come back to claim my bride."

"And her fortune, perhaps?" Lady Gunneston purred. "All the world knows that the Talbots are burnt to the socket, Edward."

"And, dear ma'am," Edward parried smoothly, "all the world knows that Devon Gunneston is a damned loose fish whose debts at the tables are astronomical, to say the least, while the late Lord Gunneston's debts—on an animal named, I believe, Blood-and-Thunder—wiped out most of Dev's inheritance." He permitted himself the smallest trace of a smile.

This thrust pierced Lady Gunneston's heavy armor. Her cold gray eyes narrowed, and it was only with the greatest self-control that she kept her seat. "You are calling my son a loose fish, sir? That is hardly polite talk for a man who wishes me to consent to his marriage to my dear niece."

"A niece whom you have just finished castigating as a hoyden? Come now, ma'am, doing it a bit too brown. If Cassandra marries me, she will be a duchess, and I doubt that her lawyers will fail to notice your refusal of a dukedom for Cassandra when compared to a mere barony—a barony to a first cousin, at that."

"All the world knows you have not a feather to fly with," Lady Gunneston countered. "Devon has an income of two hundred a year!"

Edward shrugged. "A mere drop in the bucket compared to Cassandra's income, even after you have deducted your very generous mortmain allowance, a sum that I doubt very much has been put into either her clothing or her comfort, to judge from her appearance at her own ball. Come, madam, I am tired of this game. You know me, and you know Cassandra. Will you give your consent, or must I drop around to her lawyers' office?"

Lady Gunneston's thin breast heaved and the knuckles of her hand were white against the dark wood of her chair. "Ah, but I also know—and I doubt very much if there is anyone in London who does not know—of your, shall we say, association with Lady Chantry." She was, Edward noted, almost crowing with triumph. Reluctantly, for he was not at heart an unkind man, Edward made up his mind.

"If we must talk of relationships and intimacies, Lady Gunneston, it is also fairly well known that Devon Gunneston's debts have not all been caused by gambling. There is the matter of certain injuries inflicted upon a certain very young female in a certain, ah, establishment frequented by gentlemen only." Suddenly, his voice was hard and steel-edged. "Would you like me to place that matter in plainer language, Lady Gunneston? For I will be more than happy to do so—"

"Lies!" she hissed between clenched teeth. "All lies! Jealous people, trying to ruin the reputation of my son!"

Edward shrugged. "Should the matter be brought before Peers' Trial, madam, I am certain that several gentlemen would have to force themselves to be excused from sitting jury, and called upon honor, would have to place themselves in the witness box to testify to the truth of the matter. And believe me, it is not a pleasant story to be told."

He began to draw on his gloves, carefully not looking at her face. He knew that he had thrust too close to home this time. But Edward also knew that he must remove Cassandra from this household, or he would never be able to face himself again, for after this encounter, her life would be made miserable.

Suddenly, Lady Gunneston arose from her chair and jerked at the bell rope. Her face was white and drawn with fury, her entire body trembling with rage.

With almost indecent haste, Jackson appeared in the doorway. Edward wondered if he had been listening at the door.

"Send Lady Cassandra in here at once!" Lady Gunneston commanded, keeping her voice below a shriek only with a great deal of effort.

Jackson merely nodded, and disappeared without so much as a glance at the duke.

In the few seconds that they were left alone, neither His Grace nor Lady Gunneston looked at one another. Edward suddenly found a small rent in one of his gloves to be of utmost interest.

"You sent for me, Aunt Gunneston?" Cassandra asked

timidly, peering in the doorway. Edward noted that she had not changed her dress.

"Come in and close the door." Lady Gunneston snapped.

Cassandra, with a questioning look at Edward, did as she was told. Edward stood up, instinctively placing himself between aunt and niece.

"You," Lady Gunneston hissed at Cassandra, her face a pale mask of fury. "Have you been engaged to this man for four years, as he says, or is it a lie, like so many of the things you say? I want the truth, girl!"

Edward could feel Cassandra trembling, even without looking at her. The girl's fear was thick enough to sense; Edward knew that strange, eerie sensation of terror from war. But he managed to keep himself quiet, containing his own anger.

"Yes, ma'am. It is true," Cassandra replied in a high voice, the words catching in her throat.

Lady Gunneston drew her lips back from her teeth. Edward had the strong sensation that had she been alone with her niece, she would have struck the girl. "Why did you not come to me and tell me of this before you entered into this alliance? Why did you allow me to make a fool of myself in front of everyone, of all my friends, your poor dear cousins, my dear Devon, Selene's chances ruined—" In her rage, the woman was sputtering.

Cassandra instinctively thrust her arm through Edward's and drew close to him in the manner of a puppy that has been whipped too often.

Suddenly, Lady Gunneston stopped. A slow, malicious smile crossed her face. "Very well," she said in a voice that could have cut steel. "If you are so attached to this penniless war hero, you may go with him now! Go! I do not want to see you in this house one instant longer! You ungrateful little hussy. After everything I have done for you, after the care I have lavished on you, to allow *you* to marry my own son—get out! I do not want to see your face one instant longer! You may follow your fine duke into the streets, and the pair of you the scandal of London! And don't think that I will not see to that, either!"

"Cassandra," Edward said quietly, "go and pack your things. Quickly."

With one last grateful look at him, Cassandra scurried away, her slippers making a soft sound on the bare floor. Lady Gunneston's eyes followed her retreating back out of the room, her mouth working with soundless fury. At last she threw Edward a terrible, triumphant look.

"You wanted an heiress, Duke. Now you have one! And what you will do with her, I have not the faintest idea!" She broke into a peal of bitter laughter.

Edward, totally disgusted now, turned on his heel to leave the room. At the door, he paused and looked down his ducal nose. "The scandal, madam, will fall upon your head, for I am sure that between my grandmother and Sir Geoffrey Russell-Broome, there will not be a soul in London who will not know of your conduct on this day!" Having delivered himself of this piece, he bowed coldly and closed the door upon the lady's hardened face.

Within a few minutes, Cassandra joined Edward in the hall, carrying a bandbox under her arm. Her face was pale and her green eyes were wide, but her lips were firmly pressed together, and despite the blue paint across her nose and the pelisse buttoned askew, she carried herself like a lady.

Behind her, panting slightly, Jackson followed with a small trunk, which he laid to rest on the floor. Despite his best efforts to maintain a professional demeanor, Edward could see that the butler was upset at this turn of events. Just as he was about to inquire if His Grace and Lady Cassie would like him to summon a hack, a shriek rent the air, and The Honourable Selene Gunneston, her face hidden beneath a thick layer of Miles' Cucumber Lotion, and her thin figure wrapped in a dressing gown, descended the stairway from the upper floors. "*I* was to marry the duke! Mamma said that *I* was to be the duchess, not you, Cassie, you beast! It's not fair! It's not fair! I'm much prettier than you are! I should be the duchess! You were to marry Devon, so I could be a duchess! How could you be so selfish, Cassie? It's not fair for you to be so ugly and have all that money and be a duchess too—"

Catching sight of the Duke of Woodland looking up at her as if she were a not very interesting character in a rather dull play, Miss Gunneston burst into a sustained shriek and retreated into the upper regions of the house.

Without thinking, Edward tossed Jackson a coin, shouldered Cassie's trunk, surprised at its lightness, and ushered his bride-to-be out into the cold morning light of Upper Mount Street.

As the door closed behind them, there was yet another fracas from within the Gunneston household, this one of such clarity and duration that several people on the street stopped to stare.

Cassandra turned to Edward. "I do believe that Jackson has finally given notice. I'm afraid Aunt Amelia has had a very bad morning."

The duke threw back his head and laughed. Shifting Cassie's little trunk on his shoulder, he removed a handkerchief from an interior pocket and dabbed at the smudge across her nose, then handed her the handkerchief. It was darned and slightly shabby, but she reverently tucked it away in her reticule as a souvenir of this day's work. Oblivious to the stares of onlookers, they walked down the street toward the corner, both of them slightly dazed by the scene that had just been enacted.

After a while, Cassandra looked up at the duke from beneath her lashes. His profile was hard and set, and she felt a surge of guilt. "I'm so very sorry, Edward. I didn't mean for this to happen, really I didn't."

Edward, who with considerable satisfaction had been turning his interview with Lady Gunneston over in his mind, glanced down at Lady Cassandra Russell as if seeing her for the first time. "That's all right. Carried heavier things than this in Spain, for longer distances."

Cassandra shook her head. "No, I mean having myself thrust upon you in this way."

Until that moment, it had not really occurred to Edward that he was now irrevocably responsible for Cassandra Russell's future; he had lost his accursed temper again and thought only about delivering Lady Gunneston the return fire she so richly deserved. Without slackening his pace, Edward considered this new fact. "Couldn't let you stay there," he said gruffly. "Whole household ought to be shipped to Bedlam wholesale. Daresay if you went back after this morning's work, Cassie, she'd beat you with a slipper."

"No. A riding crop," Cassandra replied earnestly.

The duke did not care to ask if she was joking or not. He had no further wish to discuss the Gunnestons, now or ever. Instead, he whistled tunelessly through his teeth, considering what ought to be done next.

Cassandra trotted along beside him like an adoring puppy. Edward, she was certain, would think of something. Edward always had, and as far as she was concerned, always would. Wonderful, perfect Edward could do no wrong, she thought fiercely. Of course, it had been very, very wrong of her to ask him to marry her. She should have asked Geoffrey, who, no doubt, would have been happy to oblige. But that foolish imp inside her had guided her to ask Edward instead, knowing full well that he would never have consented to the scheme if he had known that she had been head over heels in love with him for as long as she could remember. To Edward it was simply to be a marriage of convenience and nothing more. His sense of honor would have forbidden his marriage to Cassandra if he had known that she harbored a great tendre for him. It was obvious that he still saw her as the same little girl who climbed in trees and whitewashed the butler's coattails. Lady Chantry, she supposed, was more in his style. But, she vowed, walking along beside him, he would never, never know how much she cared about him. It was enough to be with him. And for someone who had known so little happiness in her eighteen years, Cassandra considered that simply walking aimlessly down Upper Mount Street with Edward was enough to make her ready to die then and there with joy.

"What sort of a person would I be, after all, to leave you there in that dragon's clutches? Doubtless once she

knew from which quarter the wind was blowing, she'd
have Dev running you off to Gretna. Damme, Cassie, how
did you put up with that Turkish treatment all these
years?"

"Turkish treatment?" Cassandra asked.

It occurred to Edward that she had never known anything else, and doubtless assumed that the Gunneston
household was the norm. Well, there was nothing else to
do now but marry the girl, he thought slowly. It would
be the best way to handle the entire affair, and to save
Cassandra from further scandal. His eyes narrowed.
Damned if he would allow anyone to say aught against
the future Duchess of Woodland. If Cassie had come to
him—what was the duchess' expression?—in her petticoat without a shilling to her name, it would still have to
come to the same answer. There were no certainties in
this world. God, how well he knew that now, after years
of war. But he turned his confused thoughts over; Cassie
would do as well as the next female. He'd known her from
her cradle, and he knew she would make no demands
on him.

And why, once she was set up as a married lady, doubtless she would be able to find her own way. Cassie had
always been adept at amusing herself. Well, somehow or
other it would all work out.

Having made up his mind, the duke stopped for a
moment to unshoulder Cassandra's trunk. Glad of this
respite, she also stopped, and looked around her curi-
ously. It occurred to her that she had not eaten since
luncheon yesterday. It seemed years ago, and she was
very hungry. Seeing a woman selling meat pies, Cassie
dug into her reticule for her last shillings.

Absently, Edward sat down on the trunk, oblivious to the curious stares of passersby. He rubbed his hand across his forehead, trying to sort out his thoughts.

"Would you like kidney or pork?" Cassandra said, cutting into his thoughts. He looked up to see her proffering two pastries for his inspection. Without thinking, he chose the kidney pie and took a bite, still thinking out what must be done. Serene in her faith, Cassie seated herself on the bandbox and began hungrily to devour the suety pastry, waiting for Edward to provide a solution.

The morning light fell sharply across the old houses in the square. Already the city was alive with bustling traffic and people scurrying to and fro on their day's business. Cassandra watched with interest as a butcher's boy and a chandler's apprentice jostled, then fought, for the right of way in the kennels of the street.

Finally Edward stood up and shouldered the trunk again, hailing down a hackney.

Barely waiting for Cassandra to scramble up behind him, Edward gave the hack his direction with a sense of triumph. "Temple Bar," he said firmly.

"Temple Bar?" Cassandra asked timidly, for she had been almost certain that Edward had changed his mind and was returning her to her aunt's house.

"Temple Bar," Edward repeated with a grin. "I suppose either your solicitor or mine should know how to go about getting one of those whatcamecallits, so we don't have to wait for the banns to be posted." He grinned at Cassandra. "I'm sorry, but I really don't know very much about getting buckled. This is my first attempt at matrimony. Anyway, we ought to see your man, to let him know that everything's right and tight between us, so he doesn't think I'm some blasted fortune-hunter. Which, I suppose, now that I think on it, it must appear that I am."

Cassandra's hand reached out to touch Edward's arm. Her fingertips brushed the sleeve of his coat and she withdrew again, but Edward, mistaking the gesture for anxiety, clutched her fingers briefly in his. "Don't be afraid, Cassie; once we're buckled right and tight, the old hag won't be able to touch you with a turnpike. You're safe now, I promise."

It had never occurred to Cassandra that she was anything but right and tight with her beloved Edward, and she smiled. "If Spreckles says anything, I shall simply say that I have decided it would be a good thing to be a duchess," she said more firmly than she felt. "Thank you very much, Edward. It's hard to believe that I just made my come-out yesterday, and today I'm getting married."

At precisely two-fifteen that afternoon, in the presence of the dowager duchess, Sir Geoffrey Russell-Broome, the groom's solicitor, the bride's solicitor and the very startled rector of St. John's Temple Bar, Lady Cassandra Russell became the Duchess of Woodland, wearing a hand-me-down merino dress and a pelisse with a meat-pie stain running down the front.

The Dowager cried a bit and called the bride her dear, dear child. The groom planted a light, swift kiss on his new wife's cheek. The bride's solicitor shook his head and said this was all very irregular. The groom's solicitor silently praised the fates for this reverse in the Woodland fortunes. The rector, having seen many stranger things in his day, merely pronounced the couple man and wife. Sir Geoffrey Russell-Broome, however, had the last word. After he had congratulated the groom and kissed the bride's cheek, he sighed regretfully. "Thing to do now, Cassie, is get that man of yours to sign over some money to you. Can't be a duchess in that rig. You'd be laughed out of Almack's."

CHAPTER
3

THE wedding supper was a makeshift affair at best, cooked by a chef in the sulks because he had been given no prior warning, and served by a footman and a maid almost stumbling over themselves with curiosity about this unexpected alliance between Lady Cassandra Russell and the duke. The fact that Woodland House belowstairs had received the news well before the Dowager and Sir Geoffrey—thanks in part to the housekeeper's niece being in service at the Gunneston residence—had done nothing to allay this excitement. Such details as could be gleaned only served to heighten speculation in the servants' hall.

"Kicked out the old witch's pins, our Master Edward did," the butler crowed over supper. "And brought young Lady Cassandra right out of that den of iniquity."

"It's just like one o' them fairy tales, it is," put in a very young parlormaid.

Strawbridge, the Dowager's abigail, snorted that it

seemed to her to be a very practical arrangement indeed. "Young Lady Cassandra has been kicking up larks since she was out of her cradle. But Her Grace will hear no ill of her, and that's an end on that. Here now, Mr. Kellog, pass us a bit o' them boiled potatoes." She paused thoughtfully. "Happen that Lady Cassie has a desire to be a duchess herself, and Master Edward's up the River Tick. Well, I for one don't think it's proper not to post the banns, but since the war there's been all sorts of looseness amongst them as should know better. As long as Her Grace is happy, why, I'm happy."

"Ah," said Turrett, the head groom. "And I'll lay you a year's wages there's one over on Half-Moon Street who won't be happy to hear the news either. Happen that one will be in a rare taking over this bit o' news."

"And bad cess to her," Mr. Kellog said with rare frankness, spearing a chop from the plate. "For all that she calls herself a lady, she's nought but a Cyprian. Let us hope that this will send that one packing with her nose out of joint." He raised his glass. "I give you the health of our family."

"And our new lady," added Turrett.

"Hear, hear!"

Abovestairs, the mood was almost as festive. Cassandra, scarcely able to believe her own good fortune, picked shyly at the food on her plate, all too aware of the sight she must present in that terrible merino dress. In the grand and empty dining room of Woodland House, she felt strangely out of place, particularly when the Dowager remarked that this was now Cassandra's house, to do with what she pleased. From time to time, she stole shy glances at Edward, but he was doing full justice to his dinner and barely seemed to notice she was there.

But what the newlyweds lacked in spirit was more than made up for by Sir Geoffrey and the Dowager. In keeping with the occasion, that lady told several very Georgian stories and drank, without apparent effect, the greater part of a bottle of claret. "Now that I have seen the proper thing done," she announced at the end of the meal, "I believe I shall retire to Woodland Manor for a space of time. I have always had the greatest dislike of interfering in-laws, and to tell truth, I am somewhat tired of town. Each Season becomes more deadly dull for me, as I survive more and more of my friends. Having put Amelia Gunneston in her place once and for all, I feel that I have done my duty by the family. I leave it to you, dear Cassandra, to bring Julia out next year."

Cassandra, barely out twenty-four hours herself, looked stricken. "Oh, please, dear Godmamma, do not leave! I am sure that I should not want to displace you here or anywhere!"

The Dowager patted Cassandra's hand firmly. "My dear, all married couples need some time alone in which to adjust to their married state. And," she winked broadly, "all that I need to complete my happiness would be the sight of my great-grandchildren."

"Grand'mère," Edward said softly, but the Dowager was not to be thus silenced.

With a quelling look at Edward, she continued. "When one reaches my years, one of the few pleasures left to one is the right to say *exactly* what one pleases. 'Pon rep,

Edward my love, don't tell me that you need me about this place any longer. It is Cassandra's house now, and I daresay there are a great many things she would like to do here—from attic to cellars, the place ought to be redecorated. Geoffrey, you could help Cassandra with that. Edward doesn't know a damask from a drawstring cord."

Geoffrey bowed across the table. "Always willing to lend any assistance, of course. Fact of the matter is, this place could be set to rights with a great deal of style."

After the rather flat custard had been removed from the table, the Dowager shepherded Cassandra off to the drawing room, for what Edward assumed correctly would be an even more frank discussion—this time, on the more intimate details of being a wife. He shook his head and half-smiled.

He drained off his first glass of port and lit one of his cigarillos before pouring the second glass. It was a long while before he could bring himself to look at his cousin.

"Daresay you're wondering what happened, Geoff," the duke said thickly.

Sir Geoffrey pinged at his glass with thumb and forefinger, frowning slightly at the off-tone. "People will talk, Edward. Not that you've ever given a hang for what anyone's had to say, but a lady's reputation is involved here."

"What, Cassandra?" Edward demanded incredulously. "Why, she's pluck to the backbone!"

Sir Geoffrey made a miniscule adjustment to his cravat, frowning slightly. "Perhaps so, dear boy, but Cassandra's also in a deuced awkward situation. Left her aunt's house this morning with you, married by special license, and tonight she's the new Duchess of Woodland. And the girl ain't been out a day. She has no more idea of how to go on than—well, than the schoolgirl she is. No good setting people's backs up. If she's not received, well, it could be a bad situation for her. And then there's Julia to think off on. Next year, she'll be comin' out on the marriage mart, and it would hurt your sister if your wife looked odd, don't you know."

Edward frowned thoughtfully. Here was a new and unexpected problem.

"Damn," he said at last, looking up at his friend with something akin to terror in his eyes. "Good Lord, Geoff, I've gone and gotten myself married to Cassandra Russell!"

Sir Geoffrey nodded, waiting for this remarkable fact to fully sink into his friend's head. "A good thing, old boy. But the thing of it is, gettin' married ain't exactly like a flirt, y'know. You're committed. Leg-shackled. Lady's reputation to think of. Got to see Cassie properly set up, don't you know. Thing to do, I think, is let the truth get about. Best way to do that is tell Sally Jersey. She'll make sure that no harm comes to Cassandra from any of the other old hens. Have to get her Almack's vouchers, anyway. But once Sally knows what Aunt Gunneston had in mind for poor Cassie, she'll take care of the rest, see that Cassie moves about with the right sort of people, keep the old tattlemongers quiet and all that." Sir Geoffrey looked down at his fingernails. "Between Sally and me, I believe we've enough credit on the ton to see Cassie set up properly, make sure that she don't make any mistakes or any of that. But you've got to do your part, too, Edward, old boy."

"My part! I made her a duchess—" Edward began bleakly, but Geoffrey held up his hand.

"That's all right. That's fine, and I wish you both joy. But, dash it, Edward, the thing is, you've got to take Cassie about for a while, a month or two, just until she gets the hang of things. Differences between a debutante and a matron. Married woman can get away with a lot more, of course, but still, she's got to know when to reel in the line and when she may cast out her hook. What I am tryin' to say, don't you know, is that for the time being, you've got to give Liza Chantry a wide berth."

"What does Liza have to do with Cassie?" Edward asked blankly. "You'd hardly find Liza at Almack's, after all."

Geoffrey nodded. "Quite so. But you should see Cassie at Almack's, and you should be there at least once in a while with her. I can do the rest—cousin and all that— but surely, dear boy, you weren't thinkin' of casting the girl out on the ton, cold? She has no more notion of how to go on than—"

"The schoolgirl she is," Edward finished. "I know, I know. But there are other things I'll have to attend to now, the estates, and the businesses. A lot has to be set to rights now. And surely just refurbishing this house should keep her busy for a while."

Sir Geoffrey shrugged his shoulders. He could see that his suggestions were falling on far from fruitful ground. "Well, suppose we'll just have to do our best, won't we?" he said vaguely. "But Edward, you've got to at least try. Wouldn't be fair not to give Cassie some time to find her bearings before you cast off."

The duke sighed. "Oh, very well. I shall put on that damned evening dress and squire her about among Society's fools. But you, Geoff, will have to take her to the opera. That I refuse to do."

To her credit, Strawbridge had done her best with what few things Cassandra had brought with her from the Gunnestons'. And as the girl sat up in the duke's bed, her straw-colored hair brushed into its own natural curls, and her virginal white nightdress freshly pressed, that dour abigail could not help but allow a slight smile to cross her face, remembering a time long ago when she had made the same ministrations to the Dowager, at just such a time. But, as she thought of the large trousseau the Dowager had brought with her, she sighed in pity for Cassandra. Really, the shabby condition of the child's underthings!

"If there is nothing else you would be wishing, Lady Cassan—Your Grace—I shall attend to Her Grace now."

Cassandra, too numb to speak, merely shook her head, and Strawbridge exited. On her way out, she informed the duke's man that Her Grace—meaning Cassandra—was prepared for the evening, and she went to brush the Dowager's hair.

Edward, who had been sitting in a corner of his dressing room reading a book, looked with distaste at Cassandra's trunk on the floor, and sighed. To his own surprise, he was nervous. Casting the book aside, he tightened the cord of his dressing gown and dismissed his valet.

At the bedroom door, Edward paused and took a deep breath. Then he walked into the room that had until tonight, been solely his province, his male sanctuary away from all females.

Cassandra sat in the middle of the heavy oak bed, her back straight, her hands neatly folded in the lap of the bedclothes. Her green eyes met the duke's, then dropped. She wondered if he could hear her heart thundering in her breast all the way across the room. This was the moment she had daydreamed about, when Edward could come like a knight errant to carry her off from the Gunnestons' to Woodland House. Except, as usual, reality was all wrong, for the duke was looking at her in a most odd way, not at all loverlike.

For one split infinity of a second, Edward saw Liza Chantry in her revealing peignoir, stretching out invitingly upon her golden swan bed, her arms opened wide to receive his embrace. Hastily and rather guiltily, he erased that thought from his mind and crossed the floor to the bed. Uncertainly, he paused at the foot of the stead, removing his dressing gown and tossing it, as he always did, over the post.

Hesitantly, Cassandra moved over to make room for him, terrified that he would turn on his heel and leave the room. And Edward, looking down at her, thinking how very childlike Cassandra looked, lost in the sheets and quilts, almost did.

"Edward," the new Duchess of Woodland said hesitantly, "do you sleep on the right or the left?"

This question was so totally unexpected that for the second time that day, Edward found himself laughing. "The right, Cassie," he muttered. And because the floor was so cold, he crawled beneath the sheets, surprised at how warm her little body was.

CHAPTER
4

WHEN she awoke in the morning, even before she opened her eyes, Cassandra remembered that she was a married lady now, and she smiled when she remembered the Dowager's instructions. Slowly and carefully, she turned over on her side and opened her eyes to study her new husband.

Asleep, Edward looked much younger, almost as he had before he had left for the war. His thick hair was tousled, and his long eyelashes lay on his cheeks. He slept, she noted, on his side, with one leg drawn up beneath the other, and one arm flung over the side of the bed. His breathing was deep and even. She was glad that he did not snore, although she would have loved even that fault in her adored Edward.

Carefully, lest she awaken him and allow him to find her surveying her idol in such adoration, Cassie slid out of bed and bundled herself into his dressing gown. She rubbed the soft silk over her cheek, for it smelled of his skin and the sandalwood soap he used. Very quietly, she tiptoed across the floor to the dressing room and rang the bell for his tea to be sent up, just as the Dowager had told her he liked it in the morning.

Without much fuss over herself, she dressed in her one good morning gown, a sprigged muslin with ruffles at throat and wrist, and descended into the breakfast parlor.

"Good morning, Your Grace," whispered the house-maid on the stairs.

Cassandra replied with her sunny smile and proceeded through the empty, echoing rooms. Alone at the enormous table, she pinched herself to make certain that this was all real and no dream.

A footman appeared, suppressing a yawn. "Good morning, Your Grace," he said. "Will you wish to take a look at the menus for today? The chef has sent up several suggestions for your consideration." She watched as he poured her coffee. When it occurred to her that she, Cassandra Russell—no, Cassandra Talbot—was "Your Grace," and that she was to select the menu, she blushed furiously.

"Oh, no, that is, I think the duchess should pick out the courses," she stammered.

The footman shook his head. "Begging your pardon, Your Grace, but the duchess said as how you were mistress of the house now, and you would be picking out the menus and giving the orders. Housekeeper is waiting your instructions."

"Oh, dear," Cassandra said aloud. "I've never picked out a menu in my life."

Gently, the footman presented several handwritten cards for her inspection. "His Grace is right fond of a good side of beef, and he does like his removes," the servant suggested helpfully.

In this fashion, Cassandra was able to discharge her household duties for the morning, all the while awaiting someone to unmask her as an impostor. In the Gunnestons' household, her treatment had been something less than considerate at times, servants taking their cues from their masters. Had she known with what sympathy the staff of Woodland House regarded her plight, she would have been much more at ease in her first attempts at running a house.

She was two-thirds of the way done with this chore when Edward descended to the breakfast room, and his sudden appearance was enough to cast her into confusion.

Watching her, Edward wondered if she would ever be able to run not one, but two, great houses, unaware that she had actually been doing quite well that morning before his appearance.

After she had dismissed the housekeeper, she turned to the duke and was gratified to receive a perfunctory peck on the forehead and a casual "Good morning, Cassie."

Blissfully ignorant of the havoc he was causing within her breast, Edward took his place at the table and poured his second cup of tea.

Seeing that Cassandra looked none the worse for what he assumed to have been her ordeal of the night before, he felt better on that score.

"I say, Cassie," he began after a moment's silence, "I suppose I was, well, perhaps somewhat ungentlemanly last night."

Cassandra flushed to the roots of her hair. She shook her head. "Oh, no, Edward. I'm sure I could not have— that is—it was all that I could have wished for." She bit her lip and looked down at her plate, lest she betray herself.

But Edward had not noticed, so intent was he on his own feeling that he had somehow taken advantage of her. He frowned at his teacup. "Well, perhaps it would be better if we had the Rose Room fixed up for you. It was my mother's bedroom, and perhaps you would be more comfortable there."

Cassandra's hands clenched and unclenched in her lap as she bit back the urge to protest that she wanted to stay where she was. "As you wish, Edward," she finally managed to say.

With this delicate matter cleared out of the way, the duke relaxed.

"Edward—I—" Cassandra started, but at that moment, the Dowager sailed into the room, looking almost youthful in a very fetching morning cap of Russian lace.

"Good morning, my cherubs!" she exclaimed brightly, planting a kiss on each cheek in turn. "Well, my dear Cassandra, I see you have charged the staff, and very well, according to Strawbridge's report! Never fear, my loves, it is an excellent day for travel, is it not? I daresay I shall sleep in my own bed tonight!" She spooned several generous portions of sugar into her coffee as she spoke, and looked appreciatively at the platter of sausages the footman placed before her.

"You are not thinking of leaving today!" Cassandra exclaimed. "Godmamma—"

The Dowager shook her head. "Nonsense. I came to town specifically to see you fired off, my love! And now that things have come round far better than I ever expected, I believe I should get on home and leave you two to London life. When one has outlived nearly all one's friends, town becomes rather dull. Anyway, I have some rather interesting buds coming up on my gloxinias, and my gardener assures me they will not bloom unless I am present. I do hope when I am gone that you will keep up the forcing houses, Cassandra. Now there is a place where one may blow the ready!"

"Grand'mère!" Edward exclaimed. "Wherever did you learn such language?"

"Hither and yon, my dear, and wherever." The Dowager's eyes twinkled. "Doubtless the use of cant would be considered shockingly vulgar in a mere countess and quite below reproach in a marchioness, but, Cassandra, when one is a duchess one is expected to have the greatest eccentricities."

Cassandra nodded, seriously absorbing this latest lesson in ducal conduct, but Edward laughed and threw down his newspaper. "Grand'mère, you're putting fustian notions into Cassie's head. I assure you, she can get into enough of a knot without your advice! Must you leave so soon, though? I was hoping you would bear Cassie company while I try to straighten out our affairs. A goodly job it will be, too, or so my man of business assures me."

"Please, Godmamma, it would be a great help to me, for you know that I have not the faintest idea of how to go on. I would even play piquet with you!"

The Dowager laughed heartily, but shook her head. "No, my cherubs, not even for piquet will I lay my head another night in town. I want my own bed and my own house—your house now, Cassandra, but I daresay it will take you a good year to refurbish this place. And when you turn your eye on Woodland Manor, I believe I shall rent a small house in Bath. I hear there is a goodly supply of wealthy widowers there for the picking!"

Despite their protestations and pleas, she remained firm. She was shrewd, and understood far better than they that her presence could only interfere in the delicate task of finding themselves within their relationship. Having woven her web, captured her two flies, and set that tartar Amelia Gunneston back upon her ears, the Dowager was content to allow things to sort out naturally. "And there is also Julia to be thought of, you know," she added. "I daresay when she hears the news, she will feel quite neglected in that school in Bath."

"Julia!" Cassandra exclaimed. "Oh, Edward, do you think your sister will be quite hurt that she was not at the wedding? I shall write to her at once."

"M'sister is a Bath miss, without a thought in her young head but flirting with anything in a scarlet coat, or finding some dashed awful thing to spend her allowance on. But I daresay it would be best if you wrote to her, Cassie. I'm certain she will be glad to know that you are in the family, if only because it means she can make her come out next year!"

Thinking of that lively damsel, Cassandra could only agree, but Edward had already buried his dark head in the *Gazette*, and was not, she understood, to be disturbed further with domestic issues.

After a tearful farewell to her beloved godmamma, Casandra was immediately pressed by the housekeeper into a tour of Woodland House. Since this journey involved inspecting every room from cellars to attics, and was heavily interlarded with strong hints about much-needed improvements both above- and belowstairs, from the hangings in the Blue Salon to the crying need for repairs on the leaking roof, Cassandra almost jumped with relief when Sir Geoffrey Russell-Broome was announced to be awaiting Her Grace in the Green Salon. Making her escape only with many promises to begin setting things to rights immediately, Cassandra fairly flew down the stairs to greet her cousin.

Sir Geoffrey, resplendent in pantaloons of a delicate honey hue and a waistcoat of subtle and awesomely fashionable design, was seated in a rickety chair regarding a bottle of sherry with a very critical eye. "I say, Cassie," he greeted Cassandra plaintively, pecking her cheek, "you've got to do something about the wine cellar. I wouldn't serve this swill to my worst enemy, let alone to a man who don't touch sherry before eleven in the morning."

Cassandra nodded, glancing at the clock on the mantel. "I know. Kellog has already informed me that the late duke laid down some quite inferior wines, and besides, there's an inch of water in the wine cellar, and the ceiling leaks in the underhousemaid's room, and the hangings in the blue room are rotten——"

"Not in the best of taste perhaps, but I shouldn't castigate them as rotten, don't you know," Sir Geoffrey drawled lazily, leaning on his walking stick and surveying his cousin with the same expression he had bestowed upon the offending bottle. "Marriage seems to agree with you,

Cassie. That's a very good little job of hairdressing there, but that dress should go on the rag pile."

Cassandra patted her hair. "Strawbridge did it. She says that if I only follow the natural curl, and perhaps use a rinse of henna bark, I shall come out a bit better."

Sir Geoffrey shrugged his elegant shoulders. "Be that as it may, Sally Jersey's sending over her abigail's sister or cousin or something. Says she's quite expensive and French, but knows her business. Advise you to hire her. Can't be dressing yourself, after all."

Cassandra's eyes widened. "A maid? Oh, Geoffrey, I have never had my own maid in my life! I shouldn't know what to do."

Sir Geoffrey shrugged again. "Obviously not. Could tell that just by looking at you, Cassie. Abigail does everything for you. All you have to worry about is buying the stuff. Bit of advice. Don't gossip with her, and keep her well greased in the fist to keep her yam closed. When you're up to every rig and row in town—and you should be, with me to show you the way—well, maids come in awfully handy. Deliver your *billets-doux* and that sort of thing. Accompany you to your assignations and make sure that you don't go about with rents in your petticoats, and that your library books are returned—that sort of thing."

Cassandra gave him a wide stare, but her cousin merely looked thoughtful. "Sally said to say she was delighted for you, and that she would pay a call in a couple of days. Get you your Almack's vouchers, and take you up in the park so that everyone would know that you were all the crack. Yes, have to get you a phaeton and a pair. Get Edward to pick out your cattle—he's got a good eye for horseflesh. But today's business first. Got to get you properly outfitted. Can't be seen driving in the park in that shabby gray habit of yours. Need some ball gowns, and some morning dresses and God only knows what else."

"Geoffrey, I—" Cassandra began, and her cousin looked baleful.

"Go put on your bonnet, my girl. I dragged myself out of bed at the unholiest hour of the morning just to take you to a mantua maker. She's expecting us, all the crack, you know, so come on."

If Madame Claude had known that Sir Geoffrey Russell-Broome had described her as "all the crack," she would merely have raised one delicately plucked eyebrow. In general, she was not fond of gentlemen who accompanied ladies on visits to her very exclusive and ruinously expensive showrooms on Bond Street. Gentlemen all too frequently were ready to overlook the subtle genius of her creations and make distressing remarks about the price. Not that three hundred guineas for a spangled scarf of celestial blue was inexpensive, precisely, as well Madame Claude knew. But early in her apprenticeship to the fabled Celeste, she had discovered that a fashionable woman is more likely to look and feel her very best in a garment purchased dearly than one upon which the client felt to be a bargain. But Sir Geoffrey Russell-Broome was another matter entirely. Whether he was escorting a lady of unimpeachable ton and impeccable taste, or one of his protégées from a lesser stratum of society, his instincts for the proper thing were unerringly correct. And whether the bill went to the lady's husband or to Sir Geoffrey himself, there was no matter, no unpleasantness about payment. And Sir Geoffrey, she had to admit, had done much to bring her into her current status as one of the most modish designers in London.

But when Sir Geoffrey passed under her threshold accompanied by a schoolgirl in a stained pelisse and a singularly dowdy chipstraw bonnet, even Madame Claude had to pause to consider.

Even as she rose from her Louis XV desk to greet her favored patron, she discreetly cast her eye across her engagement book. Yes, he had said the Duchess of Woodland, *née* Cassandra Russell, the heiress.

It said a great deal for Madame Claude's composure that she did not by as much as a blink of the eye betray her distress at the problem presented to her not only by Cassandra's dress, but by the female herself. Accustomed to dressing tall, slender beauties, Madame knew that her greatest challenge would be this small, seemingly colorless young thing with pale hair. Even as Madame was smiling and bowing respectfully and begging Her Grace and Sir Geoffrey to be seated, she was drawing out Cassandra's strong points—such a heavenly shade of green in the eyes, a full bosom, good shoulders, a nicely turned ankle. *Alors,* it was not much to work with, but Madame was not called a genius for nothing.

"From the inside out," Sir Geoffrey commanded, while Her Grace looked about the elegantly furnished salon with awe, twisting a button off her terrible pelisse. "Her Grace has been but, ah, recently presented, and has, ah, lived retired most of her life."

Madame Claude nodded, drawing herself up to her full height. This, she thought, was a challenge no Frenchwoman could resist. To turn this dab of a chit into a duchess could not have been accomplished by a lesser *modiste*. Sharply she called for her assistants, a bolt of muslin, a tape measure and the silk lingerie that had recently come in from Paris.

"First, Madame *la Duchesse,* the undergarments!" she exclaimed with spirit, leading Cassandra away.

"In this most delicate matter, Sir Geoffrey, *il faut que vous—comment dit-on?* trust me! *Mais, aprés cela, les robes des bals, les robes de matin, les chaussures, alors, c'est pour vous, pour votre goût!*" Madame Claude announced, clasping her hand to her breast.

Sir Geoffrey nodded complacently. Cassandra threw him one terrified look as she was led away, but he waved her on impatiently, for his eye had already fallen upon Madame's youngest and prettiest apprentice, and he had made up his mind to pass the time in harmless flirtation.

For Cassandra, who had never had more than three changes of chemise, Madame's strict injunction was slightly frightening: that no female of her rank would consider less than twenty confections of silk and lace, each one embroidered with her crest. Silk stockings at a guinea a pair, with a delicately traced clocking, Madame assured her there must be, and also *robes de nuit,* five or six, and at least two dressing gowns, one cornflower blue and, to Cassandra's eye, immodestly sheer, the other of a sea-green to match her eyes, sewn all about with *dragons à la chinoise.* Lady Jersey had ordered one very similar, of course. And not less than three corselets with the finest whalebone—and of course, Madame would be very happy to furnish *la duchesse* with the name and location of a very fine shoemaker, patronized by the most fashionable ladies of the ton, and a milliner, also quite tonnish. Cassandra's head began to spin and she surrendered herself up quite meekly, unable to believe her own transformation had already begun.

Only when Madame Claude had assured herself that Her Grace was now perfectly supplied with every essential for the boudoir did she lead Cassandra out into the main salon again, placing the girl firmly in a chair where the most exquisite creations could be brought out for her inspection.

Reluctantly, Sir Geoffrey abandoned his most interesting conversation with the pretty apprentice to turn his attention toward the outfitting of a duchess. While Cassandra watched quietly, sure that her own opinions were of no consequence in the face of two such experts, Sir Geoffrey and Madame Claude put their heads together on such matters as silks, voiles, muslins and cashmeres, the virtues of emerald versus aphrodite green, for green it must be, to bring out the heavenly green of those eyes. And gold there must be, to play up the gold of the hair, until every woman of fashion would pine that she was not as fair as the new Duchess of Woodland. Blues, perhaps, but never so deep as a midnight shade, and never so pale as to heighten a slightly rosy complexion. Never, never, Madame declared firmly, must Cassandra appear in a red, and purples—she shuddered and cast her eyes to heaven. White was for debutantes, not duchesses, although an ecru morning dress, banded at neck, wrist and hem with silk ribbands of ivory and ornamented with a delicate tracery of palest yellow daisies, would do quite nicely, both agreed.

A walking dress of copper merino, hemmed in forest

green with an overdress of that same color and fastened up to the neck with tiny copper frogs, Sir Geoffrey decided, must be set off by an enormous beaver muff and matching toque, while York tan half-boots and gloves should be added to the ensemble.

Not to be outdone, Madame Claude sent an assistant running to fetch a promenade costume, which she declared complete to a shade. Cassandra gasped with pleasure as a champagne and tangerine striped dress, topped with a mink-brown velvet redingote, was brought forth for her inspection. While Madame and Sir Geoffrey debated the shade, she fingered the orange ruching at the hem of the skirt, delighting in the smooth texture of the delicately braided silk cord. "No one else could wear such colors to advantage," Madame declared, fingering a lock of Cassandra's hair. "But *la duchesse* has the coloring, you see."

"Close to the wind, don't you know," Sir Geoffrey said vaguely. "But if she wants it, I daresay it could be brought off with the proper sort of hat. Two feathers, no more, no less!"

In rapid succession, he discarded a blue pelisse, a morning dress of appliqued rose butterflies, and a gown of dove gray with silver trimming as entirely too dowdy. An evening dress trimmed in Brussels lace was entirely too dashing, but a ball gown of pomona-green silk, with an overskirt of finest gold sarsnet, caught at sleeve and hem with tiny gold hearts, was just the thing, particularly when set off with a cashmere Indian shawl that was no more than a wisp of fabric.

But in the end, Cassandra found herself with what she

felt to be an enormous number of dresses of all sorts, and although she did not know it then, had dipped into her fortune to the tune of several thousands of pounds.

When Madame Claude at last allowed the duchess to depart her salon, Cassandra was suitably attired in a moss-green pelisse trimmed in beaver over a walking dress of cornsilk merino ornamented at hem and cuff with draped braids of moiré, a singularly elegant broad-brimmed beaver hat, trimmed with two plumes, perched upon her curls, and the merest glimpse of Russian leather half-boots visible beneath her trailing beaver tippet. Then Madame, that hardened businesswoman, was on the verge of shedding tears of pride in her own handiwork. Guiding Cassandra to the pier glass, she slowly turned the girl about so that she could inspect herself from all sides.

And Cassandra, who could not believe that she beheld herself in this mirrored woman of fashion, could only smile self-consciously with the sudden realization of her own—well, not precisely beauty, for Cassandra knew she would never be a beauty—transformation. She clapped her hands with delight, thanking Madame Claude from the bottom of her heart.

Slowly, she turned to Sir Geoffrey, who raised his quizzing glass for a long critical stare. For long seconds, both the *modiste* and the duchess held their breaths awaiting his pronouncement.

"Well, Cassie, you still ain't a beauty, but by Jove, I do believe you'll do," he said at last, dropping the glass on its string. "Knew I was right to dress you out of Madame Claude's. Handley or Celeste could never have done the job."

"Geoffrey, do you really think so?" Cassandra asked

breathlessly. "Do you think that—Edward will notice?"

"If he don't, he's a damn fool," Sir Geoffrey answered, drawing on his gloves. "Well, my girl, there's the shoe-maker and that hat woman to be seen now, but at least I ain't ashamed to so say you ain't a credit. Knew you'd do with a new rig."

After making arrangements for delivery, Cassandra and Sir Geoffrey departed. Madame Claude, totally overcome by her morning's exertions, collapsed into a chair and called for her accounts, satisfied that she had earned every penny of the enormous bill the duke would shortly receive.

Modestly dismissing Cassandra's many protestations of eternal gratitude, Sir Geoffrey left his charge on her doorstep at teatime, promising to give her a look-in within the next twenty-four hours. With one final adjustment to her hat, he made his bow and was on his way, satisfied that Cassandra's transformation from schoolgirl to fashionable young matron would add a great deal to his reputation as a man of style and taste. If Edward did not sit up and take notice of Cassandra now, he thought, sauntering down the Square, it would not be *his* fault.

Kellog, opening the door to a very tonnish young female, almost missed recognizing his mistress in her new identity. Relieving her of her bandboxes, he informed her that the master was still closeted with his man of business, that her mail had been placed in her study next to the Rose Room, and that a young person with a French accent, announcing herself as Her Grace's abigail, was even now unpacking such boxes as had arrived from her morning's shopping in her boudoir. Tactfully, he suggested that Her Grace might like her tea served in her writing room, since he had no doubt that she was exhausted from her exertions.

Upon ascertaining that all of these things met with Her Grace's approval, Kellog descended belowstairs to inform the housekeeper that Lady Cassie had come home slap up to the fives, and wasn't it just like a fairy tale, that Sir Geoffrey could make a little drab mort into a proper duchess?

Entering the Rose Room, Cassandra found a dark, slender young woman with large, liquid, brown eyes smoothing the creases out of a mound of tissue. Relieving the slightly stunned young duchess of her hat and pelisse, this young person dropped a curtsey and informed Her Grace that she was Françoise, and would be looking after Cassandra, if she gave satisfaction. Since it was clear to Cassandra that Françoise was as new to service as she was to being served, she decided they would do very well together, and left the young maid to continue to unpack and exclaim over her mistress' new wardrobe.

In the writing room, off the bedroom, Cassandra found a thick stack of cream-colored envelopes and calling cards awaiting her attention. Kicking off her boots, she stretched out upon the chaise longue and began to slit the envelopes open.

When Françoise brought in her tea tray, she found the duchess smiling at the outpouring of congratulatory notes and invitations. News, Cassandra discovered, traveled very swiftly among the Upper Ten Thousand. As she sipped her tea, she almost laughed aloud at an invitation, hastily extended for that very evening, begging for the duke's and duchess' presence at a boating party held by a notoriously toad-eating knight.

"Will madame wish to attend?" Françoise asked, stooping to pick up the discarded half-boot. "For I would suggest the voile evening dress, with the cord and lace trim."

Cassandra tossed the paper aside and stretched her toes. Pushing her fingers through her new hairstyle, she shook her head. "Oh, I do not think so. His Grace does not much care for society or parties. I imagine we will dine at home tonight. I ordered everything he likes."

Françoise smiled and nodded. "Then, if Her Grace permits, I suggest the *robe de déjeuner* with the embroidered silver slip and perhaps two or three silver roses in the hair."

Cassandra nodded, her eyes misty. "I want to look my very best, Françoise. It will be our first supper alone together. I must please His Grace in *everything*."

The little maid nodded, "Then perhaps madame should rest upon the chaise for an hour or two, to be at her freshest." As she spoke, she spread a silk coverlet over Cassandra's knees and tenderly placed a cushion behind her head. Cassandra, who was feeling sleepy after her tea, yawned and thanked her maid drowsily.

"*Dormez*, madame, and I shall allow no one to disturb you until it is time for you to dress," Françoise said, closing the door softly behind her.

At the stroke of eight, Cassandra, nervously touching her hair just one more time, descended the enormous staircase. Her slippers made a soft sound on the threadbare carpet and for the first time she found Woodland House somehow huge, silent, and lonely. As she walked down the long passageway to the dining room past the bare walls with their dark, square reminders of the paintings that had once hung there, she shivered in the stillness.

The vast Sheraton dining room, illuminated by two braces of candles, was only slightly less gloomy. The long table, designed to hold twelve, seemed to her to fill the room with its long, empty mahogany space. The silver épergne in the center dimly reflected the candlelight, and a low fire in the grate only served to add to the desolation and gloom. As Cassandra took her place at the end of the table, she noticed that hers was the only place setting, and that there was no sign of Edward.

"Good evening, Your Grace," Kellog said smoothly, appearing from the shadows with the first remove.

"Good evening, Kellog," Cassandra returned, trying to keep the disappointed quaver out of her voice. "Where is the duke?"

Kellog set the plate before her. As he expertly spooned out the tomato compote, he seemed to draw back into the shadows so she could not see his expression. "His Grace recalled a prior engagement that could not be broken. Since you had left orders that you were not to be disturbed, he asked me to convey his regrets to you and beg that you do not wait up for him, since he does not expect to come in until quite late in the evening."

Despite her every resolution to the contrary, Cassandra felt as if someone had thrust a dagger into her heart. She bowed her head, and the vain, silly silver roses in her hair glimmered in the candlelight. A footman appeared, sprinkled sugared rosewater over her compote and melted back into the shadows. Another footman poured out a soupçon of wine into her glass.

As she lifted the crystal goblet to her lips, Cassandra saw her hand was trembling. "I see," she said in a small childlike voice. "Thank you, Kellog."

"Very good, Your Grace," Kellog said tonelessly, directing a fierce look at the second footman over her head.

One by one the courses arrived from the kitchen, and one by one they returned, barely touched. Alone in the great dining room, surrounded by silent, efficient servants, Cassandra fought valiantly to keep the tears from flooding down her pale cheeks. When at last she had sent the raspberry tart away and risen from the table, she had to force herself not to run from the room.

For a while, she sat alone in the drawing room, twisting her shawl through her fingers and staring into the fire. With all her heart she wished the Dowager were here, if not to advise her, at least to bear her company through the long empty evening that stretched ahead. And after that, there would be other days and other nights, empty and endless. But she should be used to loneliness, Cassandra thought sadly. Why should that change now? Before she had always found things to amuse herself, her watercolors, her books.

But her watercolors were back in the schoolroom at the Gunnestons', forgotten in her haste to leave, and the library of Woodland House had been sold off long ago to pay the debts.

She sat for a while longer, listening to the coaches and

carriages rumbling through the streets outside. All about her, people were preparing for their evening, going to parties, dressing up, meeting friends and—lovers.

Suddenly, Cassandra stood up, unable to bear that thought. She took a turn about the room, trying to clear the thought of Edward and Lady Chantry—for that was where he must be, she knew—away from her mind.

Her turn about the room was ineffective, and she walked out into the silent hall. Faintly, from belowstairs, she could hear the sounds of the servants eating dinner— the rattle of glass against silver, someone, Kellog perhaps, telling a joke and then laughing at his own humor. That impulsive imp which dwelt within Cassandra seized her, and quietly, she descended the servants' stairs the housekeeper had shown her that morning.

The staff was seated around their table, to Cassandra like a real family, eating and talking with gusto. Here, she thought, there was light and laughter. Although the servants' hall was even shabbier than abovestairs, it had a certain homely charm that attracted her like a moth to a flame.

"So, I says, Crimshaw, I'll wager you a pint that I can place you on 'at 'ere dartboard. And bless me if he don't take me up, 'opin' it—" the second footman was saying around a large mouthful of beef stew.

Even Françoise was laughing as he gestured with his fork. "So's then, Old Flibberty comes on by, drunk as a lord as he always is on his day out, and he wants to get into the game—"

Kellog's sixth sense made him look up from the table. He rose to his feet, the smile dropping from his face. One by one, the others, sensing something wrong, followed his direction, and rose to their feet, their faces suddenly impassive and closed in the presence of this intruder from abovestairs. "Lady Cassandra—Your Grace. Is there aught amiss? I did not hear the bell."

Suddenly aware that she had committed a terrible blunder, Cassandra flushed up to the roots of her hair, backing up the stairs as if she were pinioned under their gaze, shaking her head. "Oh, no, nothing—I—I lost my way—" she murmured. And on the top step she turned and scampered across the corridor to the front stairs, running all the way up to her bedroom, where she threw herself across the rusty rose spread.

For a few minutes she hovered between tears and laughter. At first, the tears sprinkled across the spread, but because she was Cassandra, eventually she forced herself to laugh.

For a while she lay in the darkness, absolutely still. Lady Chantry, Edward, Lady Chantry and Edward, together—it ran like a chorus through her mind. And then she seemed to recall Geoffrey's voice, something about acting like a proper duchess, a married lady.

She sat up and dabbed at her eyes, wiped her nose. For a time, she sat on the edge of the bed, her knees drawn up against her chest, her arms wrapped tightly about herself. The faint glow of the gaslights outlined the heavy furniture in the room. She bit her lip.

And then she stood up and lit her candle, carrying it into the writing room. Rooting among the letters on the desk, she found the invitation to Sir Ffolkes' water party. She knew enough to know that proper ladies did not attend parties unescorted, and was about to cast the invitation away when she recalled the Dowager's advice:

duchesses are expected to be eccentric. Well, then, she would be eccentric. The Duchess of Woodland would attend Sir Ffolkes' water party unescorted.

Cassandra threw back her head, took a deep breath and rang for Françoise. With excited, trembling hands she began to undo the closures of her dinner dress, tossing it carelessly over the back of the chaise.

Catching a glimpse of herself in a small gilt mirror above the desk, she smiled. "And I shall be the most eccentric duchess of all!" Her eyes narrowed. "And Edward may have his Lady Chantry. I'll wager she's an overgrown old cow anyway!"

CHAPTER 5

LADY Elizabeth Chantry turned her famous violet eyes upon Edward's face and smiled slowly and voluptuously. As he had expected, she was pleased with the announcement of his marriage, no doubt expecting some of his newfound bounty to flow into her lap, for she was very fond of all sorts of material things, as the cluttered decor of her house testified. Edward, idly feeding the parrot from the tip of his finger, did not see her smile, but he knew it was there nonetheless.

"And you married this schoolroom chit out of her aunt's house? Whatever for? Didn't she want a proper society wedding, with all the Royals there to smile their fat German blessings?"

Edward thrust his hand into his pocket, watching the beady-eyed parrot peck at the bit of bread. A muscle in his jaw twitched, but his voice was smooth as he replied. "I had no other choice. The situation was forced upon us by her vindictive aunt. Lady Gunneston was trying to force her into a marriage with her cousin, Dishonourable Devon Gunneston!"

"And can you blame her aunt?" Lady Chantry asked, selecting a bunch of grapes from the silver bowl on the table. Slowly, she pulled the purple skin away from the delicate meat, using her long fingernails to perform the delicate operation. "Everyone knows he's been run off his legs for this past year. That affair at Mother Goody's must have cost him a pretty penny." She popped the grape into her mouth, reclining back against the profusion of cushions on the couch. When she had assured herself that Edward was watching the parrot's antics, she drew the thin fabric of her gown behind her back, the better to reveal the full curves of her form. As she raised her arms to pat her elaborate hairstyle, the heavy gold bracelets on her arms made a clanging sound. Her hands touched the heavy amethyst drops in her ears, caressed the great lavender stones around her throat, traced the fall of the necklace into the cleavage revealed by the tight, low neckline of her gown, as if assuring herself that everything was there.

Violets, Edward thought absently, looking about the cluttered chamber, everything of Eliza's reeks of violets.

When he thought of the way Cassandra smelled last night, like freshly washed muslin and the faintest trace of some light flowery fragrance, he closed his eyes, then shook his head, to remove the memory, and yes, the guilt.

"Edward," Lady Chantry purred, her mouth full of grapes, "do come and sit down. You're like some caged animal, pacing back and forth tonight. Whatever is the matter?"

He shook his head. "Restless, I suppose. Eliza, until I have settled Cassie—my wife—into her position in Society, I'm afraid that my visits here will have to be less frequent. I cannot allow any sort of gossip to affect her. Lord knows, things are bad enough as it is, with us kicking off the traces." He looked down at the gold band on his finger.

Her laughter echoed in his ears, false and strident. The violet eyes were cool, calculating. "I see. Since it is she who has the purse strings now, you would, of course, not wish to give offense."

To his own surprise, Edward felt annoyed. "It's her reputation I'm thinking of, not her money. Dammit, Eliza, can't you see? I've known her since she was in her cradle. She's had a rough time of it as it is. She deserves better than I can give her. She deserves to have a Season, even if she is married now; she hasn't the faintest idea of how to go on. If I'm not there to tip her the ready, there's no telling what sort of scrapes she'll get into. It's not as if she could do what I do, have an arrangement like ours, you see. She don't know anyone! But for a female in her position, Society is the important thing. So I've got to make my leg and truck her out to every rig and row in town."

"And what about me?" Eliza Chantry pouted, shredding the grape stem with her nails. "What am I supposed to do while you're trotting your wife about, the two of you just like Darby and Joan?"

Despite himself, Edward smiled. "Oh, I don't doubt that you'll find some way to pass the time, Liza. Hitch up that white phaeton of yours and go for a drive in the park!"

Lady Chantry laughed again. "And watch all those flash morts look down their noses at me? Oh, I know what they think of me, I know what they say about me! And by God, they're all right! Eliza Goudge came out of Goldhanger Alley and worked as a serving wench in a gaming house. And married old Lord Chantry, just before he stuck his spoon in the wall! And helped him to do it! Oh, it's true, indeed it is! And what else would you have me do? What else was I to do, I ask you? Marry some publican and have a dozen brats before I was twenty-five? Never!"

Edward, having heard this diatribe before, was not impressed. "You will recall, Eliza, when we commenced our relationship, that there were to be no tangles on either side. Each of us was to do as he or she pleased. Since it was your suggestion, Eliza, I fail to see why it should upset you now."

Lady Chantry reclined against her famous couch, nestling among the cushions and regarding Edward from beneath sable lashes. A faint smile hovered on her lips. "You are quite correct, Edward, Your Grace! If the child must be taken in hand, then you should do so immediately. And then, after you have seen her established, you may return as often as you like." She patted the sofa with her hand, enticingly. "Come, sit down and have some wine, Duke. This whole thing has made you entirely too tense. You need to relax."

And the duke, tired of his own perplexity, obeyed, throwing himself across the cushions with a long sigh. Lady Chantry leaned toward him, the fabric of her dress sighing as it slid across his sleeve. Her hand twined into his hair, her breath whispered in his ear.

He took the wine she offered him and drained off the glass.

"Later, perhaps," he heard her saying. "There is a set of rubies in the window at Burrough's."

"Cassie wouldn't look good in rubies," he said absently, throwing his head back. "Buy her emeralds or sapphires, pearls, but never rubies."

The duke did not see the expression on Lady Chantry's face. It passed like a shadow, and she leaned down to press her lips against his.

It would have been quite difficult to find any person of ton in London who could admit to *liking* Sir Ffolkes Watford, although many could claim to his acquaintance. Although it was generally known that his fortunes had been acquired in Trade, and that his tastes were not of the very best, his willingness to expend enormous sums upon the entertainment of his guests had endeared him to no less a personage than the Prince Regent. Of a consequence, Sir Ffolkes's regattas, routs, assemblies, masques and *divertissements* were always well-attended, and if the highest sticklers did not deign to grace his threshold, the guests could be counted on to be, at least, very lively.

A barge, set upon the Thames at Queen's Landing, covered from bow to stern with cast-molds covered with gold leaf and adorned in an Egyptian motif of Horus' eyes, ankhs, and heiroglyphs, tented over with panes of glass supported by pillars done in lotus motif and illuminated by five thousand candles. Each candle was held in the paws of an ebony cat set into the central structure of the tent, large enough to support a full orchestra. A platoon of servants dressed in what could have passed for Egyptian costume bore goblets of wine and trays of sweetmeats, and several hundred guests circulated on a dance floor and two balconies—and all of this was in mid-November weather. It was more than Cassandra had been used to in her life with the Gunnestons. Fortunately for her own grace, the ball was well underway when she arrived, and the absence of an escort was not noticed in the general commotion. Having never met her host, Cassandra felt no obligation to present herself to him, and feeling very much like a small child who has eluded her governess for a few hours, she cast off her opera cloak into the arms of a maid dressed in a rather astounding Egyptian headdress, and passed into the ballroom. In a gown of sea-green crepe highlighted with a gossamer overslip and embroidered seashells at hem and sleeve, her hair dressed *à la* Aphrodite and held with a fanshell pin, her feet encased in delicate slippers of pomona green and her pearl seedlets clasped about her throat, she felt quite strange, and took pleasure in knowing that several people stopped their conversations to watch her drift across the floor. For a young woman who had been castigated as a little squab and a drab chit all of her life, the experience of being admired, even by strangers, was very heady.

She took a tulip glass of champagne from a passing servant and sipped at the light bubbling wine, watching the dancers go through the motions of the boulanger with wide-eyed pleasure. How very graceful they looked, the ladies in their bright, beautiful gowns, the gentlemen in their darker evening clothes, weaving in and out of the delicate patterns required by the dance. Almost unconsciously, she tapped her foot and hummed in time to the music, drinking in all of her host's exotic display with her champagne. Since many others were wandering about in frank astonishment of Sir Ffolkes's latest extravagance, she felt no qualms about doing the same thing. One champagne glass was easily exchanged for another, as Cassandra beheld an array of sphinxes upholding an urn from which gushed rivulets of colored water, a replica of the god Set holding a flaming torch and faced with the goddess Nut, also grasping a flaming torch, the pair nearly twenty feet tall and exact in every detail. "I hear he bought them from one of Napoleon's marshals," remarked a stout *grande dame* near Cassandra.

"And had it all imported over here piece by piece," remarked her companion tartly.

Wandering along the wide galleries, Cassandra saw such an array of sun gods, sphinxes, and busts of Cleopatra that her head almost began to spin, and she felt as if she had wandered into a wing of the British Museum. Whenever her glass was empty, a servant emerged to replace it with another, and in this way she spent a good hour enjoying herself as much as if she had been at

Astley's Amphitheatre, with no other thought in her mind than the absolute wonder of it all, and if she hiccupped one time and stumbled another, she put it down to the fact that it was almost impossible for one to keep one's eyes on the ground, for even there, rich carpets had been laid down, elaborate tapestries depicting various aspects of Egyptian life.

But she was totally unprepared for the small antechamber built over the musicians' gallery, and it took a great deal of self-control for her to keep her glass clutched firmly in her hand. For in this room a *tableau vivant* had been set up, and a certain sloe-eyed opera dancer paid an enormous fortune to costume herself as Cleopatra and recline upon a couch through the evening, her arms outstretched in the act of receiving a casket of jewels from an adoring Marc Antony, enacted stiffly by a handsome young comedic actor currently all the rage at Covent Garden. All around them, other actors recruited for the evening stood in various postures; holding peacock fans, urns, pillows, baskets of fruit, musical instruments, and in one particular case, a stuffed asp.

Cassandra, stumbling upon this unexpectedly, fell back, waiting to be reprimanded for her intrusion. But when actors and actresses continued to hold their positions without moving so much as an eyelash, she watched with absorption, turning this unexpected display over in her mind. She had never been to the theater in her life; such entertainments were frowned upon severely by Lady Gunneston, but Devon had possessed a print of the opera dancer, and Cassandra was awed by coming face to face with such a celebrity in such unusual circumstances.

"Miss Mary O'Hara!" Cassandra exclaimed at last, having put the name to the face.

Miss O'Hara's lips twitched slightly, but she held her pose as the young lady moved forward to inspect her more closely. "To be sure, Miss O'Hara, I have seen the print, but imagine seeing such a famous beauty in person! Oh, you are beautiful, just as Devon said. I know you aren't supposed to say anything now—I didn't before, but my cousin Devon Gunneston says you are the most beautiful woman in England and—"

Before Miss O'Hara's very slender acting abilities could be put to their most severe test, Cassandra became aware of someone behind her chuckling, and she spun about, suddenly aware of just how very dizzy two—no, three, or was it four?—glasses of champagne could make one. She was confronted with a stout-looking gentleman in a rather questionable coat. Again, Cassandra's head spun; his face was quite familiar, but she was certain that she had never met him. At that moment, the face was ruddy and crinkled up with good humor, and that expression, she knew, was not quite correct.

"So, my dear, you have stumbled upon Ffolkey's little joke, eh? Never seen a *tableau vivant* before, eh?"

Cassandra shook her head. "Oh, no! And I am afraid that I have quite discomforted the—the players! But you see, I am not much used to going out into Society, and at home, of course, we would never have such a thing. Aunt would be shocked at the idea."

The gentleman chuckled again. "Did I hear you say your cousin was Devon Gunneston?"

Cassandra nodded, and somehow found herself walking in step along the gallery with this stranger. What harm could there be, she thought, at such a ball? "Yes, Dishonourable Dev is my cousin, although I am not precisely certain that I should call him Dishonourable Dev, except that everyone does. Edward says that he's a loose fish, but I am not quite certain what that means."

The gentleman burst into hearty laughter, causing several people gathered behind a statue to look up. Seeing the gentleman, their disdainful expressions smoothed over swiftly and they bowed in his direction.

The gentleman acknowledged the bows with a careless wave of his hand and looked again at Cassandra.

"Your Highness!" She breathed and fell into a curtsey. "Forgive me—your face was familiar, but I couldn't place it, of course, since when one is presented at Court, all the Royals look alike because one is so frightened, and the hoops get in the way, and one is certain to crush one's plumes getting out of the carriage and—oh, *you* know, of course, you must, since you are the Prince Regent!" Cassandra finished this speech with some awkwardness, flushing to the roots of her hair, but the Regent was so amused that he barely noticed. Lending her his hand to guide her to her feet again, he laughed, and she noted that His Highness' stays creaked in a most alarming fashion. "There, now, miss! Think naught on it! By God, I don't remember you amongst the come-outs this year. At least not the ones sent to Court, anyway. Most o'the mammas don't let me near their daughters, y'know." He gave her a wink.

"But I have no mamma," Cassandra replied, gently disengaging her arm from his grasp. "And, sir, we have not been properly introduced."

The Regent's laugh boomed out again. "Of course we

have. You just finished telling me you were presented at Court."

"But that was different," Cassandra objected, feeling what Edward called champagne logic. "That did not count, sir."

"Ah, but I know who you are. You are the nabob's daughter—Old Golden Ball Russell's gel—lemme see, now, I have it at the tip of my tongue. Ah! Duchess of Woodland! Why, my girl, you're the latest on-dit! Heard from that Jersey woman that your aunt threw you out of the house along with the duke because she wouldn't accept his suit! Wanted to set you up with Dishonourable Dev, and you weren't having any of it! Of course! Lor', what a story that was—wrenching, Duchess, positively wrenching! Secret engagement and all that. Touched my heart." He laid a broad palm against his chest and lowered his voice. "I too have suffered for love, you know," he confided.

Cassandra nodded. "And a very tragic story it was, sir. Why, I learned of it in the schoolroom, and we wept for you, all three of us, and my cousin Selene said it was gothic—"

"Quite so, quite so," the Regent put in hurriedly. "All water under the dam now." He looked about. "But I say, where's Talbot? Shouldn't think you'd want to be parted, after such a romantic marriage as that."

Cassandra thought hurriedly. "I—he—that is, the duke is not feeling well tonight! But he begged me to come, since I wanted so much to see the spectacle."

This set His Highness off to laughing again. He grasped two glasses of champagne from a passing waiter and presented her with one. "You know, Duchess, I'd heard you was an Original, but I had to experience it myself to believe it! Madam, may I drink to your health?"

Cassandra nodded. "I would be honored, sir. And more honored if you would drink to the success of my marriage."

One royal eyebrow raised slightly, but the Regent drank her toast.

Cassandra smiled and raised her glass with a grace she was far from feeling. "To *your* health, sir."

"Quite so, quite so. Well, I say, as long as you've managed to give your escort the slip, Duchess, would you like to take a turn with me on the promenade? Dashed chilly up here! I have the greatest dislike of drafts, you know. When I built my little pile at Brighton, I made absolutely certain that—"

Cassandra did not hear the rest of the sentence, for she suddenly noted that the royal arm was encircling her waist.

Trying to smile, she tapped the Regent with her fan. "La, sir, remember I am a married woman!" She tried to make her voice sound light, to fight the rising panic within her heart.

"And I'm a married man, don't you know!" the Regent replied, grasping her waist even more tightly within his arm. "Trouble is, Princess don't understand me."

Cassandra was desperately considering her alternatives. It would not do to offend the Regent with a reproof or a slap, in the manner one would rid oneself of Devon. Having never before found herself alone with a man who considered her attractive, she had no experience from which to draw for such a situation. She was considering a well-timed fainting spell, when she suddenly caught sight of a familiar figure strolling along the gallery, with a severely disapproving look upon his features as he studied the tapestries and frescos lining the wall.

"Geoffrey!" Cassandra exclaimed, praising her luck. "Oh, Your Highness, there is my escort, Sir Geoffrey Russell-Broome. Please, I beg of you. My husband is terribly jealous and Sir Geoffrey is his dearest friend—"

She was gratified to feel herself freed from the royal embrace. At the same time, Sir Geoffrey, hearing his name called, advanced upon them with all of his usual dignified pace, pausing only to give a moment's study to the cut of his coat of black superfine in a mirror.

"Geoff, I have been looking everywhere for you," Cassandra said swiftly, before he could speak. "I lost you in the dancers, and I'm afraid I lost my head and wandered away, and His Highness has been good enough to explain the tableau to me. So very gratifying, but I feel rather faint, and I really think I should go home to be sure that Edward is all right—so ill—"

To his credit, Sir Geoffrey immediately appraised the situation. Not by as much as a flicker did he betray Cassandra. "There you are, girl. Been lookin' for you for the last hour! Servant, Prinny! I say, ain't this the dashed thing Ffolkes has done since the time he packed us all off to the Tower for that Tudor thing of his? Never saw so much Egyptain rot in all my life!"

"Quite so, quite so," the Regent murmured. "I was just saying as much to Her Grace. Well, Geoff, must be going. Don't do to keep m'brother waitin' to play a hand of faro! Beat a few hundred guineas off him last night, and he wants his blood-and-ready back! Your Grace, I hope to see you again! Geoff—"

Cassandra watched with relief as the Prince walked away. When he was well out of earshot, she turned to Geoffrey, who was looking at her quizzically. "Now what, Cassie? Damne if I know what you're doing here! Where's Edward? Walking the gallery with Prinny! Won't do, my girl. It just won't do! Should have told you he ain't all the thing."

"The *prince?*" Cassandra asked dubiously.

Sir Geoffrey nodded. "Not all the thing at all. Dirty dish, if you ask me, and what's more, not the set you want to get involved with. Carlton house, too fast by half, even with your fortune. I say, where's Edward? Why didn't he tell you not to do such a thing?"

"Because he's with Lady Chantry and I came alone," Cassandra said miserably. "Oh, Geoff, will you take me home? I've made a wretched botch of it tonight!"

"Alone? You came here alone? Why, even the duchess wouldn't come here alone. It ain't done. And what's more, if you want to go to these things and Edward won't take you, you send 'round to me. Or anyone. But not alone."

Cassandra sighed. "Is that below reproach?"

Sir Geoffrey nodded firmly. "Quite below reproach."

They descended the stairs together. "Anyway," he continued, "What makes you think Edward's with, er—Lady Chantry?"

"Where else would he be?" Cassandra asked miserably. "Oh, Geoff, I was dressed up to the nines for dinner, and I had to eat all alone in that great big empty dining room, and oh, I'm hopeless! I shall never be a good duchess!"

"Be with his man of business. Be at a prize fight. Be

at his club. Be any one of a number of places that ain't to do with females. Daresay he went to a prize fight, or something."

"Do you think so?" Cassandra asked hopefully.

"Bound to be," Sir Geoffrey lied. "Thing to do is get you home before he gets back and finds out what you've done. Anyone asks you what you were doing here, you tell 'em. Came with me. Wanted to see the lions."

"Are there lions here, too?" Cassandra asked hopefully, looking about the great gilt dome.

"Course not! And what's more, stay away from Prinny. Dashed bad ton, that man! And that coat! Well, I ask you, would you want to be seen with a man who wears a coat like that?"

"No," Cassandra replied meekly, allowing Sir Geoffrey to fetch her cloak and wrap it firmly about her shoulders. With one small adjustment to her head ornament, he led her out into her carriage.

CHAPTER
6

THE duke was engrossed in the paper. His thin face drew down as he scanned the bleak morning headlines, and he shook his head slightly over the latest follies of

Parliament. Since he did not choose to take his seat in the House of Lords, however, he really had no one to blame but himself; after all, there was nothing to prohibit him from taking to the hustings except a singular lack of interest in all forms of political power. And this brought him around to the inescapable conclusion that he was as much to blame as anyone else for the sorry state of the world. His hand, hovering in empty air, reached around the newsprint for his teacup. Still reading, he continued to fumble for several minutes before looking over the headlines. He was surprised to see Cassandra, attired in a singularly fetching morning dress of pale ivory and silk crochet, her hair falling about her face in little ringlets from a thin silk ribband bound through her curls, filling his teacup from the silver pot.

Not at his best in the mornings, it took the duke several seconds to arrive at the conclusion that this fashionable and very attractive female was actually his wife. And even then, having seen the transformation, he found it hard to credit.

Cassandra smiled at him as she handed him the steaming cup. "Good morning, Edward," she said brightly, picking up her napkin and sliding it through the silver ring into her lap. Quite aware of his studied gaze, she carefully poured her own tea, stirred in sugar and cream, and picked up her own morning paper, unfolding it beside her plate.

Edward blinked. "Cassie?" he said, holding the steaming cup in his hand.

"Yes, Edward?" The green eyes met his innocently. "Is everything to your taste?" she asked, scanning the table anxiously.

"Yes, just right, thank you. I—er—that's a very becoming dress, Cassie."

She nodded, her ringlets bobbing like spaniel's ears. "I think so, too. Geoffrey picked it out. He says I shall be all the crack," she added naïvely. "Is it wrong, Edward?"

He shook his head, finding himself smiling. "No, no, not wrong at all. You *do* look all the crack."

"Oh, thank you. I thought perhaps something was wrong."

"Wrong?" Edward asked, puzzled.

She shook her head. "I have noticed that you do not like conversation in the mornings, until you have had your tea, and glanced at your paper. Therefore, I contrived to make as little noise as possible, and I took a subscription to *my* morning paper, for if you read, then I shall read too, and then my wretched tongue will not be a bother to you."

Edward thought this over for a moment. "I see," he said at last. "But, by God, Cassie, I wouldn't have known it was you. Your hair—that dress—you look like a different female."

"Françoise says that the proper clothes and the right hairdressing can make a great deal of difference. Her aunt is Lady Jersey's woman, you see, and she learned everything from her."

"Françoise? You mean that little creature with the French accent I passed on the stairs this morning?"

Cassandra nodded. "Her wages are very high, you see, because she trained with her aunt. But this way, her mother does not have to work for that lacemaker, for her eyes are going bad, and her brother can continue his career. He is an apprentice to a linen-draper, and some-day Françoise's mother and brother will have their own shop, and Françoise will be able to marry her coach-man."

Edward listened to this recitation with his mouth open. In all the years he had been on the town, it never would have occurred to him to ask his man about the state of his family affairs. That Cassandra had managed to glean all this information from a maid she had employed for barely twenty-four hours seemed strange to him. But if the girl continued to turn Cassie out in such an attractive fashion, he could find no complaints with her.

Cassandra waited, her hands in her lap, for his pro-nouncement, but he merely murmured that he liked a happy ending as much as the next man and picked up his paper again. But his eyes would not focus on the print; he kept seeing the transformed Cassandra before him. It was disturbing. He frowned and tried to concentrate. Incredible what difference a decent gown and an attrac-tive hairstyle could do for a female. It was as if she had been touched by magic. Must be more than that, he thought. Perhaps escaping the Gunneston household helped a great deal, but, dash it, it just wouldn't do for a man to find himself attracted to his own wife over the breakfast table! He stole a glance at her over the top of his paper.

With her golden head bent over the table and her lashes almost resting against her cheeks, one hand curled beneath her chin supporting her head, the other bringing the teacup to her lips, she was a pretty picture for a man to behold, frowning ever so slightly as she struggled with the political events of the day. "Corn Laws," she muttered to herself, as if she were in the schoolroom. "Lord Melbourne, India Trading Company, Louis XV—one, one, one—seventeenth? No, eighteenth. Monroe? Madison—"

Edward was suddenly aware of an impulse to kiss the rose spots in her cheeks. He restrained himself, however, believing that such a gesture would doubtless shock and perhaps discomfort Cassandra's composure. If he had known that such an action on his part would have been greeted with a most unseemly encouragement, perhaps he would have suited his movement to his thoughts.

Sensing his gaze upon her, Cassandra looked up, her hand going toward the teapot and the bell, anticipating his wishes. Edward indicated that he was comfortable, and was about to say more when Kellog trod silently into the room, bearing the morning mail on a salver. Her Grace's correspondence was placed in front of her; the duke picked his own up impatiently, wishing Kellog, that venerable and valued retainer, in Hell at that moment.

Like a child with Christmas presents, Cassandra ignored the cloisonné letter opener placed by her plate and slit the first envelope open with a table knife, an action the duke found strangely endearing.

"Oh, Edward, Julia writes to say that she wishes us well, you and I, and would I be so kind as to send her a pair of pink silk stockings, as such are all the rage in Bath."

She passed the scrawled note across the table to Edward, who scanned it briefly. "Certainly not," he said at last. "She has a very good allowance from our mother's estate with which to buy all sorts of fripperies. And what's more, a pair of pink stockings would make her look like a Covent Garden nun. Next thing you know, she'll want to gilt her toenails."

"Are there nuns in Covent Garden?" Cassandra asked. "I thought the convent had been pulled down years and years ago."

Carefully and patiently, Edward explained exactly what a Covent Garden nun was to this day and age. Cassandra listened carefully, and nodded. "And they really do call them abbesses? What a famous joke! Of course, I do not think that I would like to lead a life like that. It sounds very difficult."

"Undoubtedly," Edward returned drily.

"Well, I am sure that it would not be proper for her to paint her toenails gold. Indeed, I don't think I would do it, either, but I don't see that a pair of silk stockings would compromise her honor." She stuffed the note back into the envelope.

"Julia has a handsome allowance, Cassie—" Edward began.

But Cassandra shook her head firmly. "If I am as rich as everyone says I am, then I shan't send us to debtors' prison over one pair of stockings. You don't understand, Edward, what it is like to be out of style with one's peers, particularly at Julia's age. And it does help to have a few shillings to spend on chocolates and oranges."

Edward suddenly understood that she spoke from her own experience of hand-me-down dresses and an aunt with a tight hand on the purse strings. "Very well, Cassie," he said more gently. "But please, do not spoil her. Julia is already entirely too forward and headstrong for her own good, and getting to be man-mad in the bargain. I believe it takes all of Miss Goodbody's efforts to keep m'sister from eloping with a scarlet coat on half pay."

"Edward! Your own sister!" Cassandra protested, but having known Lady Julia Talbot for many years, she could find no disagreement with this statement. Even so, pink stockings, and perhaps a new cap, a bottle of jasmine toilet water, a pair of gloves, and a shawl would not be unwelcome in Bath. Cassandra made a mental note to take Françoise to the Pantheon with her, to purchase just such items. Having been wretchedly poor all of her life, Cassandra found most gratifying the idea of being able to expend her generous heart upon her friends.

There were several congratulatory notes, more invitations, and the promised vouchers from Almack's, together with a few words from Lady Jersey. All of these were duly passed on for Edward's inspection. Cassandra also received a letter from the Dowager, addressed to Cassandra and Edward, expressing the hope that they were getting on well in London, although the weather was wretchedly wet, and that she was pleased to be beside her own fireside once again, having labored mightily to be sure that her gloxininas were all coming into bloom at once. Cassandra cast her eye over that beloved handwriting, noting the details of the Dowager's active life with awe. A rout ball here, a card party there, and the squire's son to be married to Miss Alpert in January, Miss Coldstone's influenza coming on at its usual anniversary, although dear Cornelia was holding up well, the Dowager had been nursing her friend through with elm-bark tea and mustard poultices. The Reverend Mr.

Parrot, the elderly (and, it was rumored, dipsomaniac) vicar, was showing an unfortunate tendency to appear in his cups at the dinner table, but other than that, all was well at Woodland Manor.

Cassandra had barely finished skimming through this epistle when Edward arose from the table. "I say, Cassie, would you like to give Almack's a turn-in this evening? I see Sally's sent your vouchers. And perhaps tomorrow night, we can go to the Haymarket. *Paul Pry*'s on the bill, and it's a comedy. I though perhaps you might like that."

"Of course, Edward. That is—if it's not taking time away from your—" Cassandra broke off, flushing.

"Oh, no, Cassie. This is our time—that is, it's only proper that you should be seen occasionally in company with your husband."

"Of course," Cassandra replied tonelessly. "As you wish, Edward."

Above her head, he frowned, wanting to reach out to her, but he stopped himself. "Of course, Cassie, if it don't suit you—"

"Oh, no! That is, it would suit very well."

"Then, rig yourself out and we shall dine at seven, if that is convenient."

"Edward!" Cassandra called as he left the breakfast room. Half-hopefully, he returned and stood by her chair, watching as she dipped her finger into her cold tea, tracing patterns into the tablecloth.

"I have something to tell you. I did something very wrong yesterday."

His brow rose slightly, and he waited.

"Well, last night, when you were not here for dinner,

I—I went out with Geoff to Sir Ffolkes's water party. It was quite something, really, all those sphinxes and gold platings, and a *tableau vivant* with Miss O'Hara as Cleopatra, and—well, in the crowd, Geoff and I became separated, and I wandered away, looking, you know, at the lions, and quite by accident, I ran into His Highness, and well, if Geoff had not suddenly appeared, I fear it would have been most unpleasant."

"Good God, Cassie!" Edward exclaimed, suddenly jealous. "I don't mind you goin' out with Geoff, but whatever you do, stay away from Prinny. He's not to be trusted, y'know, with a pretty woman. That was a foolish thing to do, Cass. Remember, you are the Duchess of Woodland, and not a chit of a schoolgirl anymore. You would do well to look lower to conduct your flirts, Cass."

She bowed her head. "Indeed, it was very stupid of me, and I shan't repeat the experience. He was odious!"

"See that you don't," Edward said stiffly, almost shaking with fury at the Regent's conduct. Imagine attempting to take advantage of an innocent female.

Cassandra, feeling that his anger was directed toward her, merely nodded and hung her head, listening to Edward's footsteps as they crossed the hall.

Shortly thereafter, she heard him call for his hat and greatcoat, and then the door closed behind him. She sighed and propped her head upon her hand.

Promptly at ten, Lady Jersey's card was delivered to Cassandra, as she sat at her writing desk trying to compose a suitable letter to her sister-in-law. Glad to be relieved of the task, she immediately went downstairs to receive her most important ally, and the two ladies spent a comfortable half-hour discussing the possibilities for refurbishing the main salons of the house. Lady Jersey decided that the Blue Salon must be done in teal damask, and gave Cassandra the name of her draper.

After precisely one half-hour, Lady Jersey rose to take her leave, impulsively bestowing an embrace upon her young friend and pronouncing herself very touched by Edward's choice of a bride.

Meeting Sir Geoffrey Russell-Broome on the doorstep, she remarked that the new duchess was no diamond of the first water, but she was definitely an Original, and as such would probably make herself all the rage within a very short space of time. Complimenting her old friend upon his exquisite taste in outfitting Cassandra, she took her leave, and, full of the news from Grosvenor Square, immediately paid a call upon Princess Lieven.

Sir Geoffrey, understandably touched at this compliment to his talents, was in a very good mood indeed when his cousin received him, agreeing to demean himself by a visit to that vast and crowded emporium of every sort of bargain known as the Pantheon Bazaar, in company with his cousin.

If Cassandra found herself in awe of such an establishment as Madame Claude's, at the Pantheon she was quite at home; for it had been the governess' custom to escort the young ladies of the Gunneston household to this establishment in order to teach them the precepts of economy. Such was the popularity of this shop that all members of the citizenry of London intermingled freely in their search for the *bon marché,* and Cassandra, in her gage-green bonnet and pelisse, trailing an enormous beaver muff over one hand, cheefully vied with cits' wives and sewing girls to paw through the merchandise stacked high upon the counters. While Sir Geoffrey watched in amazement, Cassandra found a length of sprigged muslin for one and six, a very fetching little morning cap of percale for two shillings, several lengths of brightly colored ribbands and two bunches of paste flowers, all to be had for three and six, while a sovereign bought her not one but three pairs of the pink silk stockings Lady Julia had so urgently requested. As Cassandra triumphantly bore her treasures to the counter, Sir Geoffrey felt a tug at his sleeve, and turned to behold Eliza Chantry, clothed from head to toe in her favorite lavender, smiling up into his eyes. "Run to the dogs, Geoff?" she teased, her eyes glittering.

"Hardly, m'girl, hardly. Accompanying the new duchess on her rounds. I say, how long has this place been here? Did you know that here you could buy a fairly decent set of smallclothes for a monkey?"

Lady Chantry laughed. "Women will always seek out a bargain, no matter how wealthy they are, eh, Sir Geoffrey?"

The dandy frowned. "Her Grace was shopping for some small items for her sister-in-law in Bath."

"I see. How very domestic of Her Grace. Is that her, over there with the sandy hair and the blue cap?" Lady Chantry pointed to a very dowdy-looking female struggling to choose between a length of sarsnet and a woolen shawl.

Geoff shook his head. "No. Her Grace is seated at the counter, in the green, don't you know."

Liza Chantry's violet eyes took in Cassandra with

some surprise. She pursed her lips and narrowed her eyes, missing no detail of her rival's dress or demeanor, from the bronze plumes in her bonnet to the little suede half-boots upon her feet. Mentally, she calculated the cost of the beaver muff and the pelisse, noted the profusion of wheat-colored curls, the retroussé nose and the wide, innocent green eyes. With a carefully indifferent shrug, she turned away. "I see. Well, His Grace's wife is—very young."

"Already bein' touted as the new Original. Lady Jersey predicts she'll be all the rage. Prince himself took a fancy to her t'other night."

"Prinny." Lady Chantry dismissed that former flame with a shrug of her shoulders. "Well, how very interesting. And now, dear Sir Geoffrey, if you will excuse me, I must be going." The dandy watched as she turned on her heel and disappeared into the throngs of women.

Coming to Cassandra's side, he found her looking after the lavender figure with interest. "Sir Geoffrey, who was that?" she asked slowly, her fingers twisting through the strings of her reticule.

"Lady Chantry," he replied briefly. Cassandra was already half up from the chair, craning her neck to catch a glimpse of this most interesting person who could capture Edward's affections. "Which way did she go? Oh, I just must see her! Is she very beautiful? They say she has lavender eyes and raven hair."

Sir Geoffrey's hand came firmly down on Cassandra's shoulder, pushing her back into her chair. "You stay where you are, Cassie, and no tricks, mind you. You're not even supposed to know that she exists."

Cassie sighed. "But I would so like to see her, just to *see* her, I wouldn't attempt to talk to her or anything improper, really, I wouldn't, Geoff. I would just like to see—what he sees in her. . . ." Her voice trailed off wistfully, and Sir Geoffrey started.

Good God, he thought, dumbfounded. She's in love with Edward! This idea was such a profound shock to him that he felt forced to sit down beside her. It cast things, he thought, into an entirely different light. He remained wrapped up in his own thoughts until the harassed clerk behind the counter presented him with Cassandra's purchases, neatly wrapped in a package.

It hardly bore thinking of! Really, Cassandra in love with Edward. And what, he wondered were Edward's feelings toward Cassandra? Lord, it could turn into a merry muddle and no mistake, unless something happened very soon. Liza Chantry was not noted for her patience.

By dinnertime, Edward had managed to control his desire to land his Prince Regent a solid facer. After an afternoon spent at Jackson's, where he had managed to take out a great deal of his frustrations on a boxing-bag, he felt a good deal better, and was almost looking forward to another evening at Almack's. Tonight, he reflected, would be different from all previous nights, for tonight, he would be escorting Cassie. Thinking of her excitement at her first visit to that establishment, he smiled.

But when Cassandra descended the stairs in her dancing dress of deep pine green trimmed in white lace, drawing on her gloves as she walked, he found himself unable to think further. As she came into the dining room, he caught the light, sweet scent of her cologne and frowned at his own feelings, puzzled. As he took his place opposite her at the long table, he noted that the candlelight softened the rosy glow of her skin until it was almost luminous, and that she had a certain trick which was absolutely charming, of inclining her head ever so slightly to one side.

Even as he mouthed pleasantries over the plates, he found himself wondering if he was falling in love with his own wife, with short, plump, freckled little Cassie Russell, who climbed trees like a boy. But this was not the Cassandra Russell he remembered, he realized. Geoff had been right. While he was gone, time had not stood still; his childhood bane and friend had slowly grown into a woman. All she needed was the right clothes, the right hairstyle, the right setting to push her over the edge of adolescence into the first bloom of womanhood.

Even when Cassandra managed to upset her wineglass, Edward barely noted, and was certainly unaware that only a few days ago, he would have been roughly calling her down for her clumsiness. But tonight, even that gesture seemed to be part of her charm, one of the little imperfections about her, which he was coming, much against his own better judgment, to cherish as a part of her.

When he found himself laughing at some chance remark of hers, it struck him that since she had come into the household, he had begun to laugh quite a bit; not at her, as he might have done when he had been up at

Eton, but with her, in a way he had not been able to laugh since the war. She could make him laugh; that in itself was a rare gift.

But what was he to do with these unexpected feelings? Cassie had married him to be a duchess, to have the parties and balls and gay life to which her fortune and birth entitled her; just out of the schoolroom, she certainly would not want to lead the quiet sort of life he had grown accustomed to in these years of poverty and war. Perhaps she would find another man, someone who would turn a proper leg and take her out to every rig in town, a young man of her own age and outlook. And then what? He would, of course, give her a divorce, if she wanted it, and lay the scandal against himself, as if it mattered what the world thought of him. But at the mere whisper of an idea that he might lose her, Edward felt an unaccustomed anxiety.

"Tell you what, Cassie. Tomorrow, we'll have a look-in at Tattersall's; get you a good pair of cattle and a proper phaeton to drive around the park." He heard himself saying.

Cassandra's eyes lit up, not so much at the thought of having a phaeton and pair as the idea that Edward would take her somewhere in his company. "I should like that very much!" she exclaimed. "Oh, that would be famous above all things!"

Edward smiled at her delight. He was about to suggest that they might abstain from going out that evening and spend their time alone together when the clock on the mantelpiece struck the quarter-hour.

Cassandra rose from the table. "We dare not be late,

Edward. They close the doors promptly at eleven, and not even Wellington himself can get in after that."

With a sigh, the duke rose from the table, ready to do his duty.

Not always privately, the duke had frequently castigated Almack's as nothing more than a slave auction. True, that august establishment, supervised by its eagle-eyed patronesses, was officially organized as a place where ladies and gentlemen of the highest ton assembled for the purposes of dancing and conversation, and also true that no beverage stronger than orangeat and no game of chance more dangerous than piquet was played. True, among its members Almack's included a great many persons already firmly bound in matrimony; *but,* the duke thought glumly as he preceded his wife up the steps and gave over his cloak and walking stick to an attendant, there always seemed to be a cursed lot of milk-and-water misses there, escorted by their mammas, all of them on the look-out for an eligible husband, that prize around which their first Season revolved. In his previous visits, the duke had dutifully danced with such females as the patronesses presented to his attention, for not even the serious lack of fortune could discourage them from believing him to be a matrimonial prize of the first stare.

A dukedom, after all, was a dukedom, and many a mamma had counseled her daughters to look as high as they pleased in selecting a mate. But the duke's disdain for Society had soon driven him away from those portals, for he was not a man who enjoyed being held up as a sultan's buyer in a Turkish auction of pastel damsels.

Accustomed to a certain amount of notice upon his arrival at any important social function, Edward was slightly surprised when, within a very few minutes of his entrance, his duchess was immediately claimed for one boulanger, two country dances, and a waltz by young men whom he privately castigated as striplings and youngjacks, fresh upon the town with the roses still in their cheeks. But as Cassandra shyly made them known to her husband, he discovered that they were her contemporaries, friends made while she was under the aegis of the Gunnestons. That to a man they were dull dogs indeed did not remove his sense of bewilderment that he must write his own name upon his wife's program in order to claim her for one waltz. He watched sullenly as Cassandra was led away by Lord Reginald Ashcroft to take her place in the set then forming. She was looking very handsome indeed in her pine green gown among the pastel debutantes.

That she threw him an apologetic glance over her shoulder, Edward did not notice. And if he had known that these gentlemen had barely noticed Cassandra in her incarnation as plain Lady Cassandra Russell of the Gunneston household, a lesser luminary beside her brighter cousins, it still would not have eased his very definite feelings of jealousy.

With a nonchalance he was far from feeling, Edward took himself off to the card room for a rubber with the other bored husbands and papas. Here he was able to agree heartily with Lord Jersey and Edmund Drummond Burrell about women in general and wives in specific, as they cut him into the game.

For Cassandra, the experience of walking into a room and being surrounded by young gentlemen eager to claim her hand for a dance was a novel experience indeed. Having always been the shadow maid among her brighter, more strident cousins, she had long been used to receiving only the most indifferent attentions from these same interchangeable young men who formed the Gunneston sisters' beaux. That she had never considered any of them worth the powder it would take to blow them away (as Edward always said) did not figure in her pleasure at having them vie for the privilege of fetching her a lemonade or standing up with her for a quadrille. Indeed, after so many years of polite indifference, it was gratifying to watch them scramble to pick up her fan or fetch her shawl from the cloakroom, particularly when she noted, from the corner of her eye, her cousin Selene, in palest pink, smiling determinedly at her from Wallflower Corner. With a slight nod of her head that sent the silver spangles in her hair dancing beneath the candlelight, Cassandra allowed Freddie—or was it Lord Reginald?—to spin her about, so that all the world could see that the Duchess of Woodland was a fine, light-footed dancer. As well she should have been, she thought, from the many hours she had practiced alone in her room while Selene went out to parties and routs. And always, as she twirled alone before the glass in the dark, cold bedroom, Edward and only Edward, fighting somewhere in Spain, had been her invisible partner. And though she laughed and bantered with them, these young men were only *temps-passants,* and meant no more to her than a dancing master, for soon Edward would claim his waltz. A waltz in Edward's arms at Almack's, as the Duchess of Woodland. It had been her deep and secret dream for many, many years.

So, Cassandra smiled at Alphie, Freddie, Reggie, Jack, and Willie, secretly amused at their tongue-tied amazement that Lady Cassandra Russell—little Cassie!—had bloomed overnight into a dashing creature with spangles in her hair and a very fashionable gown. And even though she could not remember if she was dancing with Freddie or Jack, all of them interchangeable in their very same waistcoats and inane chatter about Oxford, boxing, the watch, and horses, she was still female enough to feel a very definite sense of elation at receiving so much attention from the opposite sex.

But her partners were not limited to that sophomoric set of Gunneston beaux. Enjoying this spectacle enormously, Lady Jersey soon had made the duchess acquainted with my lords Rotherham, Ardmore, Halstead, and the Honourable Mr. Raske, and it was all Cassandra could do to excuse herself from one more country dance in order to give her satin slippers a rest. And even then, she found herself surrounded by admirers vying to pick up her fan or hold her dance program while she sipped at her lemonade, and tried to catch her breath, her green eyes dancing merrily as she uttered what she knew to be the most outrageous statements, only to hear the attentive laughter of her courtiers.

Within the space of half an hour, she found herself promised to go driving in the park with Sir Hugo Devereux, who was known for his prime cattle as much as his aversion to taking up females in his high-perch phaeton, to view the Turner exhibition at the Royal Galleries with Lord Ardmore, to take an early morning ride upon any one of Mr. Lovatt's horses that should suit her fancy, to accept an invitation to attend a military review of the 89th Scots Light Guard with Colonel Sir Harry Mac-Phearson, to go boating on the Thames aboard the Earl of Courtland's yacht, and to so many other adventures and amusements that she barely knew how she would keep them all in her mind. Intoxicated with so much attention and heady with her own success in this first venture in Society, Cassandra recklessly promised to accept every invitation, adding that, of course, she would have to have the duke's approval. But even that statement was greeted with laughter, as an example of the duchess' wit, for what matron would seek her husband's approval for any excursion she would care to make with one of her loyal courtiers?

Cassandra's court had been established, and no female wishing to shoot herself into the ton could have wished for a more illustrious set of gentlemen to dance attendance upon her whims. There was not a man among them who could not lay claim to some redeeming virtue or outstanding talent for which he would willingly offer the duchess his services and expertise, be it selecting a pleasure craft to be kept on the river at Woodland Manor, or instructions in the fine art of playing faro for guineas a point.

Edward had just laid down his cards and collected his winnings from the last rubber when Lord Ardmore wandered into the card room. "I say, Woodland!" that gentleman greeted his old friend. "Her Grace has devastated the field; the debs have called retreat, and the patronesses will have to muster their flanks if they wish to squeeze the foot-soldiers back into the front! Original! My dear Woodland, your duchess is an absolute Unique! Allow me to congratulate you on keeping her hidden away from all of us! If I'd but met her a week earlier, I'd have given you a run for your groats!" Ardmore slapped Edward heartily on the back and ambled away.

Edward managed a thin smile. "If you gentlemen will excuse me, I believe I promised m'wife a dance," he said, rising from the table.

"Better get her while you can, my boy!" Lord Jersey sighed, shuffling the pasteboards once again. "Or I daresay the bucks will carry her off on their shoulders!"

Edward found himself wading through a large group of attentive males reluctant to separate themselves from proximity to Cassandra. And his wife, in the center, seated on a chair, laughing at a particularly witty shaft from Lord Petersham, was barely aware that he stood before her, until he cleared his throat.

"Oh, Edward!" she cried, her eyes alight and her face glowing. "Shall we have our dance now?"

"If you can spare the time," the duke said, his voice much colder than he intended it to be, aware that all eyes were upon him. Carefully, Cassandra arose, retrieving her fan from one gentleman, her shawl from another, and her reticule from yet a third.

The laughter had deserted her face as he led her out onto the floor. "Oh, I did not mean to displease you, Edward," she murmured quickly as he put his hand around her waist for the waltz. "I hope I did not do anything improper, but they all came to me, and Lady Jersey was kind enough to introduce me to everyone and—"

The duke felt like the greatest gothic monster in creation, looking into her eyes. He shook his head. "No, Cassie, you are in no way offending me, I promise you.

After all, you should be setting up your court." He tried to keep his voice light as he spun her about the floor, surprised at the way in which her body responded to his directions, moving beneath his merest pressure through the strains of the music. Although he did not particularly care for dancing, years with Wellington had forced him to become an expert at that art, and for the first time, he felt as if he could take pleasure in that exercise with this female in his arms.

Cassandra closed her eyes and hummed the melody under her breath, ever so slightly off-key. Her hands resting lightly on his shoulder and in his grasp, seemed to stroke him like butterflies' wings, and for those brief moments upon the floor, he almost fancied that he knew what it was like to be in love.

They said nothing to one another, for their bodies said it all for them; together they might have been alone in the room, for all that anyone else mattered.

When the dance was over, they applauded with the rest, their eyes afraid to meet lest their secrets be discovered one by the other. But when Cassandra put her arm into Edward's so that he might escort her off the floor, he bent down and whispered in her ear.

"Would Her Grace care to go home, leaving behind a trail of broken hearts, or would she care to stay until the very end and attempt to gratify all her admirers with a dance?"

Cassandra glanced quickly at Edward's face, but she could not read his expression. Thinking that he was tired of this place, she quickly agreed, for she did not want to tax his patience further.

In the carriage, they were both silent, but Edward's

hand grasped hers in the dark, and she could feel the pressure of this thumb against the fine bones of her hand. Sinking back into the upholstery, she put her head on his shoulder and waited for the rebuff, however gentle, that she thought he would deliver. But Edward did not draw away.

"Do you like being a duchess, Cassie?" he asked the darkness.

"I like being your—that is, I—it is very nice, Edward," Cassandra said, cursing her wretched tongue for almost betraying her, and deeply grateful for this sign of his approval. If she could not have his love, she thought, at least she would always cherish his friendship. "Thank you for taking me to Almack's."

"Slave auction! Can't blow a cloud, whist for chicken stakes, a great gaggle of old hens gossiping at each other —" He broke off, laughing. "But I daresay you enjoyed it, and that's all that matters, Cassie."

"I met a great many people. I have been engaged to do a great many things, but I think I shall beg off."

Absently, Edward stroked her hair. "Cry off? Whatever for? Lord knows you deserve to have some entertainment, Cassie. You've made yourself up quite a cult, tonight."

Cassandra bit her tongue to keep from blurting out that she would see them all in Hell if they made him uncomfortable.

"Look!" Edward exclaimed, pulling back the curtain. "It's snowing! The first snow of winter."

"Oh!" Cassandra exclaimed, watching the large white flakes floating down past the streetlights into the darkness. "I have always loved snow. Aunt Gunneston used to be so put out with me, for I was always walking in the snow and ruining my boots. I think it was because Selene used to come along and would catch cold."

Edward pulled the cord. Before Cassandra could protest, he was out of the carriage into the street, pulling her along with him. "We're only a block or so from the house, but come, Cassie, and we'll walk in the snow and ruin our boots!" He lifted her away from the step and into the street. "It will be just like it was when we were children, do you remember?"

Heedless of her thin satin slippers, Cassandra spun about under the gaslight, watching the delicate white flakes pouring from the London sky. As the coach rumbled away before them, Edward wrapped Cassandra in his evening cloak and they walked slowly through the thin white blanket, hand in hand, watching their footprints on the sidewalk.

Edward lifted his face to the light. "When I was in Spain, neckdeep in mud and blood and lead, I used to think about a good English snowstorm. And sometimes I wondered if I would ever come home to see one again."

Cassandra squeezed his hand to indicate that she understood. "Sometimes, late at night, when the house was very still and cold, I would wake up, and I would listen to everyone else sleeping, and I would wonder if you were all right, if you were warm, and getting enough to eat, and—safe. I always wondered if you were—safe."

"Safe enough," Edward said drily. "Oh, there were times when I was sure that I'd seen the last of this world, when my horse was shot out from beneath me, or when I turned to see Cobble—he was my friend, Cobble was, a young fellow from Hertfordshire, just had his commission —I turned, and his body was there, but his head—" he stopped, took a deep breath. "Sorry, Cassie, I don't want to upset you. It was as if I had to close off all my own feelings, you see, just to stay alive. If you thought about it too much, on the front lines, you'd go mad."

Cassandra nodded, shivering inside her cloaks. She did not tell Edward that the Dowager had shared his letters with her, that she knew far more than he thought about the bloody horrors of Spain.

Edward sighed. His arm rested lightly across Cassandra's shoulders, as if for support. "And here we are now, you and I, safe in England. Sometimes I don't quite believe it when I wake up in my own bed in the morning, and I know I'm home in England." He looked down at the top of her head, where snowflakes nestled among the spangles. "Cassie, I want you to be happy." He said suddenly.

Cassandra stopped in her tracks and looked up at him. Her nose was red with the cold. "I am happy," she said simply. "Are you?"

They turned in at the iron fence and walked up the steps. As Edward opened the door, he turned to look at her. "Yes, Cassie, I am happy too." He brushed a snowflake away from her nose. "Would you like a glass of sherry, or should we go up to bed?" he asked, as Kellog opened the door.

"Sherry first, please. I am chilled to the bone," Cassandra said.

"Beg pardon, sir," Kellog said as he took Edward's

cloak and folded it over his arm on top of Cassandra's peusse. "But a note arrived for you during the evening."

"Really?" Edward said, taking the envelope from the butler's hand. "Cassie, run along and ring for the sherry, I'll join you as soon as I read this."

"Very well," she agreed happily, turning away to give Kellog directions.

When he heard the door close, Edward tore the seal away from the envelope. Frowning, he scanned through the familiar handwriting.

> EDWARD—(it said)
> SOMETHING TERRIBLE HAS HAPPENED. PLEASE COME TO ME AS SOON AS YOU ARE IN. I AWAIT YOU ANXIOUSLY.
> E. CHANTRY

"Damn!" he exclaimed aloud, just as Kellog emerged from the library. He crumpled the note into his pocket. "Kellog! My cloak at once, and summon up the carriage; I must go to Half-Moon Street at once!"

Cassandra, standing in the door of the library, caught the words Half-Moon Street, saw Edward leave the house and shut the door.

When Kellog brought in the sherry and some vague excuse about unexpected business, he found Cassandra dry-eyed and pale, but very calm. Almost too calm, that worthy thought shrewdly. Ah, she knew what the ready was and no mistake!

But Cassandra merely bid him set the sherry upon the table.

Well, she thought, staring into the fire, if that's the way it's going to be, then two may play at that game! I cannot fight her. Her grip on him is too strong. But I shall contrive to amuse myself! Every penny I spend on my own pleasure is one penny less she shall see in her coffers!

"Damn her!" Cassandra said aloud. And then the tears began to fall, as slowly and silently as the snow outside.

CHAPTER
7

As was his invariable and very discreet custom, Edward dismissed the hackney at the corner of Fellows Alley and Half-Moon Street, proceeding on foot through the silent, white city to Eliza Chantry's door.

Until he raised his hand to the brass fox mask on the door-knocker, he had not thought any more about the situation than that a friend had called upon him to act in an emergency; his years with Wellington had taught him to respond immediately to any distress signal, and consider the consequences later.

Yet, as the duke stood shivering in his thin opera cloak upon the stoop, waiting for Eliza's venerable butler to emerge from the servants' hall, he noted two things that gave him pause. One, there appeared to be a set of male footprints upon the snowy stoop; they went in, but did not come out again. And two, the house was dark. Not so much as one taper flickered in any of the front windows. Perhaps it was the night, or perhaps the uncharacteristic urgency of Lady Chantry's note, but Edward began to wish that he had taken his Manton down from its place above his bureau, and stuck it into his pocket, just in case. There was something havey-cavey about this business and no mistake, he thought, frowning as he heard the slow shuffle of the butler from within the house.

The bolt was drawn back and the door opened a crack. By the light of the flickering tallow stick, Edward was just able to discern Partidge's nightdress. The old man's face, never a handsome countenance, looked as mussed as the bed he must have roused himself from to answer the door.

"Milord, the household is asleep," Partidge whined through the door.

Edward opened his mouth to reply when the elderly servant began to close the door in his face. Swiftly, he placed his shoulder against the wood and pushed inward until he was almost touching Partidge's face with his own. "You will be good enough to let me in. I will see Lady Chantry immediately!" Edward's voice was that of a man used to commanding other men; with a great show of reluctance, the door swung back on its hinges and Edward came into the hall, peering about in the darkness.

"Ha' la'ship's gonna baid, I doan' knaow iffen I sheen waken ha—" Partidge sniveled dubiously.

Edward threw a coachwheel at him. With surprising agility for one so old, the butler caught it deftly, tucking it into a pocket of his shabby dressing gown. Recalling that set of footprints on the front steps, Edward's eyes narrowed into cold gray slits. "I will not leave until Lady Chantry sees me. You will be good enough to inform her of that fact," he rasped.

Muttering over his shoulder, the butler left the duke standing in the hall. The old man proceeded slowly up the steps, bearing away the only candle in the house.

Edward grunted with disgust and felt his way into the front room, a tiny cubicle euphemistically called the Lavender Salon. With his own firewheel, he lit the candelabra on the table and sat down in his wet boots to wait her appearance. The room was cold, and silent. From above, he could hear the butler knocking on Eliza's bedroom door, then low murmurs.

With a tight-lipped smile of satisfaction, he sat back to wait, annoyed at the thick stench of violet cologne that hung in the air.

In a few minutes, Lady Chantry herself, her dark hair disheveled and her voluptuous form wrapped in an elaborate nightrobe embroidered with violets, came into the room. "Edward, really, what is the meaning of this?" she asked, yawning.

Edward did not rise. "The note you sent around informed me that you were in the greatest danger, Eliza," he said in measured tones. "And begged me to wait upon you at once."

She stared at him from her great violet eyes, half-awake and yawning. "Note? What note? I wrote you no note, and if I did, I would not send it to your house where your wife would see it."

From an inner pocket, Edward produced the crumpled paper. Still yawning, Eliza took it from his hand, scanning it quizzically. Shaking her head, she handed it back to him. "It does look rather like my handwriting, but I did not write it, Edward." She pushed a curl behind one ear, and he noted that she still wore her amethyst drops.

"Is all well, then?" he asked in an undertone, scanning the dark hallway.

"Of course all is well!" she snapped, coming to life. "If I did not know you, Edward, I would accuse you of childish tricks. But it is not in your style. Obviously, one of your friends thought it was a great joke to call you out on a night like tonight." She sank into a chair, as graceful and sleek as a cat, even when only half-awake. A silver slipper tapped at the carpet in annoyance. "If that is all, then I suggest you go home to your wife and allow me to return to my bed." She yawned again. "I would ask you to stay, but tonight I want only to sleep—alone."

Edward took the note. "A joke! A jest! And doubtless some young fop is collecting his fifty-guinea wager even now! If ever I catch the man, I will call him out."

"Yes, do so! Only not tonight! I have taken my laudanum drops, and I am in no mood to be merry and laugh," Eliza Chantry said sulkily. "If that is all, Edward, I bid you good evening. Please come again when I am suitably prepared to receive you." She gave him her sleepy half-smile, holding out her beringed hand. "A man should not see his mistress when she is not at her best. It destroys all the illusions so necessary to love-making."

Edward forced himself to return her smile and take her hand. "As you say, dear ma'am," he forced himself to reply with equal cynicism. "I will show myself out. Pray forgive me for intruding upon you in this fashion."

Standing far from the streetlight, he watched as she blew out the candle in the Lavender Salon. At the same time, someone in the bedroom parted the curtains and looked out into the night. Edward could not see the face, but he defined the shape to be masculine. His lips twisted. So Eliza chose to entertain others? He walked slowly away toward Suffolk Square, where there was a hack stand, turning this over in his mind. Of course, it did not bother him that Lady Chantry chose to have other lovers —theirs was no binding love, as all the world knew. But still, someone, perhaps Eliza herself, wanted him to know that she was entertaining another. Or was it something else?

Turn the matter over in his mind as he would, he could still find no answer for the night's work upon his arrival at his own door. Only then did he think of Cassandra. Letting himself in with his latchkey, he saw immediately that the library was dark and empty, and he felt a stab of guilt.

That tore it, he thought to himself as he took up the candle and ascended the stairs. I shall go and make a clean breast of this night's work to Cassie, and I will promise her that I shall not see Eliza Chantry again. Shouldn't bother Eliza too much. She seems to already have found a new partridge for the plucking, and I imagine that a handsome deposit into her accounts will satisfy her. But Cassie—good God, what have I done to Cassie? She won't like it above half that I've been out to Eliza's house in the middle of the night. But if I can just explain—if she's waiting up for me. . . .

He turned away from his own door and proceeded down the hall toward the rose bedroom. As he put his hand to the knob, he noticed how cold the metal was.

Slowly, he turned the brass globe; but it did not turn. Cassandra had locked the door. For a moment, he thought of knocking, then decided against it, sadly turning toward his own room.

In the darkness, Cassandra lay in her bed and listened to his footsteps. Then she turned over and buried her face in the pillow, muffling the sobs that threatened to break her heart.

The duchess did not appear at the breakfast table the next morning. When he asked after her, Kellog replied that Her Grace had given orders that her breakfast and newspaper be delivered to her on a tray at ten, since she did not wish to rise before that hour.

At precisely noon, when Edward was working on his accounts in his study, he heard Cassandra descend the stairs and greet Lord Ardmore. "It is a great deal too very kind of you to help set up my stable, Lord Ardmore," he heard Cassandra say, and just caught a glimpse of her fawn-colored riding habit as she swept out the door on the arm of that military man. "I would like a high-perch phaeton and bays, I think."

At four o'clock, she returned, ascended the steps to her room and closed the door. A short while later, Françoise came scurrying up the stairs, calling over her shoulder to the second footman that Her Grace would not be dining at home tonight, but was engaged to take supper at Lady Yarborough's with Sir George, then to a loo-party afterwards.

Edward ventured to knock on Cassandra's door a short time later, but it was Françoise who answered his summons, with a severe look resting upon her dark features. "Her Grace is lying down from the morning's exertions, sir. She has purchased a phaeton and pair and expects them to be delivered this evening. She says should you wish to equip yourself with suitable cattle, you have her leave to do so." Françoise dropped a curtsey and gently but firmly shut the door before Edward could protest.

He was in the library when he caught a glimpse of Sir George in evening clothes, escorting Cassandra, in a gold ball dress, out the door.

Edward dined alone at the long table that night, and for the first time since he had come into the title, he found the house intolerably empty and dull. After irritably sending two courses back to the kitchen and drinking most of a bottle of wine, he refused dessert and took himself off to his club, which seemed very thin of company that night.

After two hands of faro, he growled at his companions and left, walking home through the slush with such a dour look upon his face that not even the linkboys cared to ask if he wanted a light homeward.

Her Grace was still out, Kellog informed him impassively as Edward handed his hat and coat over to that staunch minion. The duke hurled a most uncharacteristic curse at his man's head as that worthy undressed him for bed, and the latter remarked belowstairs that it appeared that His Grace was running foul of the duchess' cannons, and no doubt. Having served the duke through the wars, he was given to the use of military cant. Françoise, knitting a shawl for the second underhouse chambermaid, remarked that Her Grace was *malheureux,* for all her triumphs. Kellog harrumphed and picked up his paper, allowing as how it all had to do with a certain female in Half-Moon Street. A footman from the Millbourne residence across the street, visiting with one of the maids, pricked up his ears.

The duke, happily unaware of these comments, settled himself in bed with Miss Austen's latest work. Under normal circumstances he found Miss Austen's prose could always elevate his spirits considerably, but tonight the words seemed to blur on the page, and he was staring at the ceiling, chewing on his lower lip, when he heard the duchess enter her own room. The candle by his bedside guttered and died, and he rolled over to try to sleep.

Over the next few days, the duke and duchess formed a cold, unspoken truce; upon those few occasions when both dined at home, they pursued only the most banal topics over the courses, and separated immediately after the meal, the duke to the library, the duchess to the drawing room, only to meet by chance upon the stairs at the end of the evening. But if Edward looked up from his books to hear Cassandra's melancholy little tunes picked out upon the pianoforte, or Cassandra sat still in the empty room, listening to the rustle of the pages, neither one gave the other any indication. Edward's stiff Talbot pride, hardened by years of humiliating poverty, and Cassandra's schoolgirl sensitivity, fostered by years of clandestine romantic novels, separated them like a vast ocean.

Upon the few occasions when they met to discuss the refurbishing of the house, Sir Geoffrey Russell-Broome was always present; and if that unfortunate dandy frequently found himself being asked to translate the utterances of one of his cousins to the other, while both were seated within inches of one another, he was too polite to make any mention of the considerable discomfort this state of affairs placed him in.

Mondays would find Woodland and the Original rigidly seated in their box at the opera, and alternate Fridays found them at Almack's, where the duke was always careful to claim the first waltz with his bride before retiring to the cardroom, to leave the field open for what was becoming known as the Original's Flock. But if a hostess sent a cream and gilt-bordered invitation to Woodland House, she knew that only the duchess, accompanied by a member of the Flock, would attend; the duke, as was well known, did not care for fashionable gatherings. But still, rumors spread through the ton, and the Woodlands were pointed out to young ladies and gentlemen as the unhappy result of notions so foolish as love matches.

While Cassandra appeared in the park in one of her riding habits, whip-points thrust into her lapel like a member of the Four-Horse Club, Lord Ardmore beside her turning her into one of the most credible female whips in London, Edward rode his magnificent gray on the bridle paths, and if they chanced to meet, duke and duchess would accord one another nothing more than a fashionable bow. But after the yellow wheels of Cassandra's phaeton had rumbled away, Edward would turn and look after her in a very strange manner, half-proud, half-furious. And as he rode on, he would find himself nursing a most uncharitable jealousy against his old friend and comrade in arms, Ardmore. Ardmore, after all, was a confirmed bachelor who had never so much as taken a mere female up in his own rig, let alone deign to instruct such a green one as Cassandra in the fine art of taking Hyde Park Corner on a wheel.

At Jackson's Boxing Saloon, Edward was startled to find that noble Corinthian, Mr. Raske, always carried one of Cassandra's stray gloves in the inner pocket of his waist-coat as a good-luck charm, going so far as to tuck it into the waistband of his trews when stepping into the ring, for he swore that only the influence of the Original had al-lowed him to get past Mr. Jackson's defenses and plant that worthy professional with a facer.

Even when Edward visited White's, where custom for-bid the mention of a lady's name within those hallowed halls, he discovered no less a neck-or-nothing gamester than Lord Rotheham, known to drop and pick up fortunes at the table without turning a hair, could and did oblique-ly refer, quite respectfully, to his progress in instructing the Original in the art of playing both deep basset and faro for golden-stakes—to win, of course, for what gentle-man of ton would deprive the Original of one single shilling of that vast fortune? That this pronouncement did not cause Lord Rotheham to be severely censured, and provoked only an awed silence from the other players, did nothing to increase this friend in Edward's eyes.

When Sir Geoffrey encountered his cousin in the Green Room of the Royal Theatre, among the bucks and opera-dancers, he sighed that it was worth as much as he had to be able to escort Cassandra to the comedies; he was greeted with an abrupt rejoiner, the like of which he had not heard since Edward's Eton days.

Sir Geoffrey lifted his quizzing glass to study the brief

costume of one particularly well-turned ingenue. "Doing it a bit too brown, don't you know, Edward," he remarked.

The duke sighed. "I suppose I am, Geoff, but damme, every time I turn about, Cassie's involved in another one of her knots and tangles! She dropped five hundred pounds at a whist party last night!"

"A drop in the ocean, dear boy. And it frightened her so badly that she was trembling when I brought her home. Gal never had more than two shillings at a time—believe that brought it home to her that she wasn't cut out to be faro's daughter."

"You ought to speak to her," Edward muttered, thrusting his hands into his pockets.

Sir Geoffrey's brow went up. "Ought to speak to her yourself, Edward, if only once in a while. Cassie's come too near to going off the deep end once or twice—those whip-points, for instance, too dashing by half. I mean, a man don't want to thrust his nose in where he's liable to have it cut off, don't you know, but it looks as if you and Cassie ain't exactly smellin' of April and May." Sir Geoffrey stretched out his leg to look critically at his black silk breeches under the light. "I wonder if a corbeau color wouldn't suit better. Must speak to Weston about it."

Edward had too much sense not to see the point of Geoffrey's remark, but he merely shrugged. "Cassie's doing exactly what she pleases, and that was the bargain we struck. It's her fortune, Geoff. I can't stop her from dropping the ready at the cards, or wearing whip-points in her lapel, or wearing through three pairs of dancing shoes in a week."

"Ought to try, dear boy," Sir Geoffrey replied. "I say, do you like this tie? I call it the Original, after Cassie."

Edward merely grunted and rose to take his leave. It was that night that he resumed his visits to Half-Moon Street, where he was not plagued by morning calls, invitations, drapers, cabinetmakers, *modistes,* painters, jewelers or the Original's Flock. There, at least, he found some semblance of peace and quiet and a female who was willing to listen to him.

A female brought up under Cassandra's circumstances would have to have had a heart of stone, not to enjoy the fashionable swirl of attention which surrounded her present circumstances. And believing with all her innocent heart that Edward had bestowed his undying affections upon Lady Chantry, that he wanted nothing to do with her beyond paying her the minimum of attention due his wife—in the manner of the late Lord Gunneston and his lady, and indeed, every other married couple she had known—she found her new position a consolation. That she, perhaps, did not enjoy her triumph as much as she appeared to seemed to her to be a very light price to pay to be near Edward. Having never known love in any of its forms, she could not recognize its hints from her husband's behavior. Just as Edward would always, in some space of his mind, regard her as little Cassie Russell who climbed trees and got into knots, so Cassandra would always see Edward as a distant hero whose indifferent crumbs of attention she treasured. That they had both grown up and matured in their viewpoints, that what existed between them was much more than the casual friendship they pretended to share, seemed beyond her wildest dreams. It was too easy for Cassandra to view

Edward's growing affections for her as lucky instances. For even at the height of her popularity, her own self-image left her no room to believe that she was truly a handsome woman, with a great deal of warm generosity and sharp wit, who could endear herself to others.

So she felt as if it were someone else who moved through an endless succession of routs, balls, parties, entertainments, morning calls, afternoon rides in the park, visits, and pleasures of which she had only dreamed before. And when she would catch herself enjoying a dance or a compliment or an outing on the Thames, she would think of Edward, and that sharp prick of pain would have the power to deprive her of happiness, only to cause her to throw herself even more fervently into an empty search for escape.

If she knew—and it would have been impossible for her not to know—that Edward was again calling in Half-Moon Street, she gave no indication to anyone, not even to Sir Geoffrey, that she was deeply wounded. Telling herself that she should feel no pain, that she had been mop-headed enough to walk into her own trap with her eyes open, she sought consolation from thought by keeping herself busy and occupied.

When she was not being entertained, she was at work on the house, slowly turning it through its stages of shabby, faded glory, through that terrible tunnel of half-stripped wallpaper and workmen's tools and Holland covers, to the days when a room was completed, fresh and vital. Here was the place where her love was reciprocated, for the house seemed to respond to her care and affection like a living thing, turning itself from a gloomy mausoleum into a home, full of life and light and brightness. With unerring instinct, she toured antique merchants and furniture-turner's warehouses, pulling dusty, forgotten things out of the attics with her own hands, kneeling with a workman to watch as the parquet was inlaid into the floor, seizing a rag from one of the maids to polish a forgotten chair back to life.

With Sir Geoffrey in tow, she went to Southeby's and bid furiously for a gentleman's entire estate, in order to return the Holbeins to their proper places on the drawing room walls. She descended upon both Turner's and Constable's studios and bore away paintings of an awesome thunderstorm at sea and a verdant landscape of Dedham Vale to hang in the dining room. The ragged carpets were ripped up from the floors and replaced with the finest Chinese tapestries she could find. A pair of lovebirds was purchased from a Portuguese sailor and allowed to fly through the conservatory, nesting among the ficus trees and Chinese ivy she placed there. Only the knowledge that Edward would issue a most strenuous protest prevented her from purchasing from the same source a small and very temperamental dog to carry about on her muff. But nothing could restrain her from ordering fresh flowers to be placed in every room, and Kellog, with tears in his eyes, was permitted to select the fine wines that were laid down in the newly white-plastered cellars.

Only Edward's room remained untouched. But even there, Cassandra could not resist making improvements. With the aid of the duke's man, the ancient mattress was replaced with a new one, and the cracked washbowl and pitcher replaced with an identical new ironstone version. If Edward noticed these changes, he did not mention them, but his praise of the rest of the house was tinged with surprise. He had not expected Cassandra to have a very good sense of style and a flair for what was both elegant and comfortable.

"I don't believe it, Cassie! Wherever did you find the Holbeins again after all these years?" he asked one evening at dinner.

Cassandra stared at him down the long table. He looked small at the other end, almost lost in the ancient ducal chair.

"At Southeby's. I bought them from Younge's estate. I thought the duchess might enjoy seeing them hanging in their proper place."

"I see." Edward nodded. He pushed a bit of curry around his plate, trying to think of something else to say.

Cassandra looked down at her napkin in her lap and drank her wine, wondering why she could talk to those who mattered little but could find no conversation for Edward.

"Are you going out tonight?" he asked.

She nodded. "To Lady Ombersley's. With Geoff. I daresay it will be a sad crush. York is supposed to put in an appearance, so I imagine it will be that sort of an odious evening where one comes home with a dreadful headache." She watched as Kellog refilled her glass. "And you?"

Edward made a wry face. "I'm engaged to go to Covent Garden." He did not say with whom, but Cassandra believed she could guess that even at that moment, Lady Chantry was preparing her domino and loo mask.

Sir Geoffrey Russell-Broome looked with slight distaste at the black silk domino he carried over his arm.

Perhaps a sage brown would have been better, he thought with a trace of regret. He glanced in the mirror over the mantelpiece, thought he saw a gray hair among the russet, pomaded locks and immediately absorbed himself in the task of plucking it out.

"Geoffrey! Whatever are you up to now?" Cassandra demanded, coming briskly into the room with her own domino of emerald green already drawn around her shoulders.

Abashedly, Geoffrey drew himself up, smoothing up his coat. "Thought I saw a gray hair, don't you know. Couldn't have that."

"Oh, let me see!" Cassandra exclaimed, immediately reaching out to ruffle her cousin's carefully sculptured locks.

Sir Geoffrey drew away in horror. "Get away! You'll get powder on my waistcoat, and that would never do!" he said indignantly. "Anyway, what's the idea, Cassie? Sending around to tell me to bring my domino. No one said anything about Lady O. havin' a masque—"

Cassandra, having admired the emerald green in the mirror over Geoffrey's shoulder, removed the domino and cast it so carelessly into a chair that her cousin winced. But even that astute critic had to admit that Cassandra was looking her very best in a gown of cream-striped satin, with thin ribbands of emerald running through the pattern, trimmed at hem and about the slashed full sleeve with satin knots of emerald and ivory. Ivory slippers embroidered with butterflies and a gold *jétterie* in her hair completed her toilet. About her neck she had clasped an emerald amulet on a gold band. Had he known that even at that moment the redoubtable

Françoise was collapsed in triumphant exhaustion in her mistress' boudoir chair, he would not have been startled. He raised his quizzing glass to his eye and nodded his approval. "Dashed fetching!" he pronounced. "A shame to waste it on such a deadly affair as the Ombersleys'." Even as he spoke, he saw the defiant gleam his cousin's eyes held, and he shook his head. "Oh, no, Cassie, not one of your dashed scrapes, gal—"

The duchess sat down in a chair. "Oh, no. Not a scrape, really, Geoff, I promise you, it will be the simplest thing, really. I have always wanted to see Covent Garden, and Edward is such a very dull stick that he will not take me."

Sir Geoffrey shook his head firmly, appalled. "Well, I ain't taking you, gal, and what's more—"

Cassandra turned wide green eyes upon him. "Then I shall send a note to Freddie, or Jack—or yes, Lord Ardmore."

"You ain't goin to Covent Garden with Ardmore! Smells of horses! And those other young fops ain't the proper people to escort you through the pit, either. Wouldn't know how to go on with a duchess in tow. Wind up losing you, and Edward would have to call 'em out," Sir Geoffrey said in measured tones of horror.

Cassandra smiled. "Then you will take, me, Geoff? Oh, you are so very good to me, you know. I should have married you instead of Edward, I knew it."

"God forbid!" Geoffrey said simply and reverently. Suddenly, a thought struck him and he removed his handkerchief from his pocket and began to mop his brow. "Cassie! You ain't fixin' to go to Covent Garden to meet anyone, are you?" he asked awefully.

"Of course not! Will all of London have me set up with a lover?" she demanded. "Of course, if I should happen to run into my husband and Lady Chantry there—"

"Cassie! Doing it a bit too brown! Cheltenham tragedy! Scandal!"

"Fudge!" Cassandra replied tartly, drawing on her gloves. "I would simply like to see the fireworks, and the abbesses, and the masks, and perhaps have a glass of ratafia, and if you should see Lady Chantry, you will point her out to me and then I shall go home, like a good girl."

"Won't do it!" Sir Geoffrey said firmly. "The idea is bad ton enough, Cassie, but, really, don't you know—"

"I shall send for Freddie then. Freddie's always one to kick up a lark! He'd come running. Dear Geoff, I promise I shan't as much as lift a finger to put Edward's nose out of joint! If he wants to appear in public places with that purple heifer on his arm, then let him make a cake out of himself. I should simply like to see her, that's all. And the fireworks, and the dancing bears, and the nuns—"

"You won't see any nuns if I can help it. For the last time, Cassie, will you put this notion out of your head and come along to Lady O.'s party like a good girl?"

"No! And no, and no!" Cassandra said firmly. "I've allowed you and Edward, and Aunt Gunneston and Lady Jersey and almost everyone else in London, to tell me what to do, all of my life, and for once, I am going to do *exactly* what *I* want to do!" She spoke with such vehemence that Sir Geoffrey was startled back into a chair.

"I say, Cassie!" He began to protest, but she turned her face away, shaking her head angrily. Two bright scarlet spots appeared in her cheeks, and her jaw was firmly set.

"Damn! And damn again!" Sir Geoffrey said angrily. "If I get anything on my coat, Cassie, I'll make you buy me a new one. Fifteen minutes! Then we go to Lady Ombersley's party."

To his great consternation, he was borne down upon by his cousin and a kiss was planted on his cheek. "Oh, Geoff! You are the dearest person alive!" Cassandra exclaimed breathlessly.

With a great deal of difficulty, Sir Geoffrey extricated himself from her embrace. "There now! I daresay you've ruined m'cravat, and it took me two hours to get it just right! Mind you, one glimpse, and then we leave and go on to Lady O.'s! Not at all the thing, don't you know, to be spying upon your husband!"

Cassandra swore there would be no deviations from the rules her cousin laid down, but there was a glitter in her green eyes, which, Sir Geoffrey could not help but feel, boded ill for the success of their clandestine project. "Mind you," he said terribly as he made adjustments to his cravat in the mirror above the fireplace. "One false step, Cassie, and it's out on your ear, my girl!"

Cassandra drew the emerald domino about her shoulders and threw back her head. "Geoffrey, you should know me better than that!"

Sir Geoffrey threw up his hands and admitted defeat.

CHAPTER
8

OF all worldly pleasures available in London, Lady Gunneston had always been particularly disapproving of the revels held at Covent Garden, stiffly hinting to her offspring and her ward that these masked balls were little more than an excuse for every sort of debauchery and decadent license, patronized by every class of society. Since this view was echoed by mammas far less conservative than Lady Gunneston, Cassandra descended from her carriage with the distinct feeling that she was about to enter into nothing less than an orgy.

While Sir Geoffrey mumbled angrily under his breath as he paid out two and six for admission and a box, Cassandra stood on tiptoe to look over his shoulder, seeking a glimpse into the Opera House, hoping to snatch a view of forbidden activities.

"Here now, none of that!" Sir Geoffrey snapped, hitching her domino firmly down over her dress. "Anyone who knows you would be able to spot that gown a mile away!"

Meekly, Cassandra allowed him to make the necessary adjustments to her mask, sustaining his grumbling as they were led to their box by a *maitre d'*, impervious to the frenzied beckonings of a gentleman in complete Tudor garb who sought to catch his attention, or to the rather openly displayed charms of a lady, dressed in a Roman toga, leaning against the column. Doing her best to look as if she was used to coming to revels every night of her life, Cassandra accepted the chair offered to her and allowed her escort to castigate the overworked waiter for handing them soiled lists. While Sir Geoffrey painstakingly procured their supper and a bottle of passable wine, Cassandra took a deep breath and peeked about, looking for signs of decadence.

She was not disappointed. The enormous, brightly lit room, hung with colored Chinese lanterns and garlands of rather venerable silk flowers, was as full as it could hold with partygoers from every segment of society. While many had chosen to appear in costumes as astounding as a red satin Mephistopheles or a Versailles milkmaid, the majority of revelers were disguised only by dominoes and masks. Far from confining themselves to the supper boxes which lined the sides of the room, most of them seemed to have saved their spaces only by dropping off their wraps before circulating along the dance floor, or conducting themselves to the boxes of perfect strangers, where they were free to flirt most outrageously under the protective coloration of their masks. An orchestra, set upon the dais at one end of the room, ground out the strains of a popular country dance, and waiters circulated through the crowd bearing tray after tray of arrack-punch, claret, or ratafia. Cassandra was certain that it was not at all the sort of place she would wish to come by herself, as she watched a young woman in a canary-yellow domino shamelessly encourage the attentions of a masked buck across the floor. Then she had the satisfaction of seeing the buck and the canary-yellow domino greet one another, share a bowl of arrack and slip away into one of the secluded alcoves which bordered the walls. Cassandra was doubly glad for Sir Geoffrey's escort, particularly when a very foxed young man in an ill-fitting Hussar uniform leaned across the partition and demanded her hand for the dance then forming. One hideous stare through Sir Geoffrey's quizzing glass was sufficient to send the Hussar on his way with a mumbled apology.

By then, their wine had arrived at table, followed by an indifferently prepared and served meal of grilled lamb in mushrooms, a remove of apple dumplings, two dishes of steak-in-blanket, a trifle of brain and kidney together with a dish of chutney. Sir Geoffrey sighed over the frugality of this repast, but Cassandra, who could only pick at her food between stares about the room, barely noticed, so intent was she upon the progress of a family of enormously large persons, obviously from the bourgeoisie, all of them barely covered with dominoes in every shade of the rainbow, making their way across the floor to take their places in a box already occupied by their friends, who waved glasses and chicken drumsticks in the air, loudly cheering their procession through the dancers. Just as it seemed that all of them could not possibly cram into the small space provided for them, their friends jovially made a press and the stout daughter of the house, with a definite switch of her ample hips, took up the last few inches of the bench, only to be immediately claimed by a gentleman wearing a law clerk's robe in lieu of a domino, and led off to the dance floor amid the bawdy calls of the clerk's companions from their box high in the tier.

Cassandra watched, wide-eyed, as a woman in a very low-cut gown, her scarlet domino thrown open to expose her form to better advantage, a scatter of rather tawdry plumes in her hair, leaned across the partition and made a most improper suggestion to Sir Geoffrey, who fluttered her away with his napkin. The woman shrugged and made a very naughty comment as she moved on to the next box, where she was greeted with more enthusiasm by a single gentleman left temporarily deserted by his own partner.

In the row above them, a party of rustic would-be Corinthians, obviously down from university on holiday, were determinedly and quite improperly conducting a flirtation with a table of rather vulgar-looking females. They were somewhat loosely chaperoned by a pock-marked, black-dressed older woman, who, in language so strong that Cassandra blushed beneath her mask, loudly called them all to order whenever she had determined that they had overstepped the rather loose lines of her propriety.

Beside them, a family party of the most respectable-looking cits, all of them neatly attired in uniform black silk dominoes, calmly went about the business of eating their dinners as if they were at home around their own board. When the largest shape, who Cassandra thought to be Papa, drained the last of the claret and slid slowly beneath the cloth without anyone's taking the slightest notice of his indisposition, she decided that this was indeed a very mad, bad place, and that she would not have missed these sights for all the ton parties of the Season.

Sir Geoffrey, who had last attended a Covent Garden revel in the company of a very young, very fresh milliner's apprentice some years ago—when he was in much the same state as his female companion—had long since ceased to find the Opera House a scene of excitement. He ate a great deal of the lamb, which he pronounced sadly underdone, drank a great deal of wine, which he declared to have lost a great deal of its bouquet by improper storage, and amused himself by ogling several of the more passable females who promenaded beneath the box. By the time he had called for a second bottle, however, his spirits were somewhat restored, partly by knowing that his idea about the brown silk domino had been quite correct, and partly by a final remove of a most excellent brandied peach cake *flambeau*. As he sipped his wine, he even unloosened so far as to demand of Cassandra if she were enjoying this crack at the lions and the geeks, a theatrical term he had but recently acquired from a certain very charming little opera dancer.

When Cassandra demanded to know what he meant by that, it cast her back into his bad graces for several minutes; when she had to be reassured that the brandied peach cake *flambeau* would not incinerate her hair, however, he was restored.

"Daresay you've seen enough, Cassie. Had dinner, now go on to Lady Ombersley's, don't you know," he suggested, tweaking his lapels.

"Oh, no!" Cassandra exclaimed, recalled reluctantly from the most interesting drama being enacted at the next table. The abandoned gentleman's companion had unexpectedly returned to the table in time to find a strange female perched upon her escort's lap. "I haven't found Edward yet, or Lady Chantry."

Mentally cursing the tenacity of Cassandra's mind, Sir Geoffrey sighed, and made a great pretense of scanning the crowd. "Daresay they didn't make an appearance. May have gone on to the theater instead, don't you know."

Cassandra, searching in vain for Edward's figure among the dancers, was forced to agree to this possibility, at last. As their waiter emptied the last of the second bottle into her empty glass, she realized that she had had a great deal more to drink than she had previously thought.

"Just goes to show you, don't it?" Sir Geoffrey said affably as he paid the shot. "Go to jumpin' conclusions, get yourself into all sorts of situations. Daresay when we toddle in from Lady Ombersley's, you'll find Edward snug in his bed after a night at the club. Daresay he ain't been near Lady C. for months."

As he spoke, he was bringing Cassandra to her feet, tucking her wrap about her shoulders, adjusting her domino again, firmly but deliberately leading her away from the table and out toward the door—he hoped, in the direction of Lady Ombersley's party.

But Cassandra craned her neck about the room, scanning from table to table, almost desperately in search of Edward, even as Sir Geoffrey was tenderly escorting her toward the portals. They were not more than ten feet from Sir Geoffrey's relief when Cassandra thought she spied a familiar tilt of the head beneath a certain domino of corbeau. She clutched dramatically at her cousin's arm, and he felt his heart sinking down to his toes as he followed her gesturing arm to the secluded grotto behind the boxes where the unmistakable pair of shoulders sat across the table from the lavender domino.

Before Sir Geoffrey could restrain her, Cassandra was away, with a purposeful stride in that direction. Although he hastened to follow her, his progress was several times impeded by females interested in gaining his attentions who had to be almost forcibly thrust out of his path.

But he was too late. Heady with wine and given Dutch courage by weeks of anger, Cassandra had already arrived at the table.

As Sir Geoffrey sought to push his way through the party of merrymakers anxious to include him among their number, he watched in horror as the unhappy pantomime unfolded before him.

The emerald domino drew up before the corbeau and the lavender, both of the latter turning. As Geoffrey watched the dark domino's shoulders stiffen, for a moment he hoped that it was a case of mistaken identity, that Cassandra would receive a much-deserved set-down and turn back to him in confusion, vowing never again to repeat the incident and begging to be taken to Lady Ombersley's party.

But this fond hope was not to materialize, for the corbeau domino had risen to a full and unmistakable height, and was even now confronting the emerald.

With effort no one would have suspected he possessed, Sir Geoffrey broke away from his inebriated captors and made for the table, praying that he could forestall trouble before Cassandra made a most regrettable cake of herself.

Almost breathlessly, he arrived on the scene just as she

was lifting her head toward Edward. The lavender domino leaned back in its chair, enormously amused, no doubt, by this spectacle.

"Why a wife should not be allowed the same privilege as her husband, if she sees fit—" Cassandra was saying over the mad strains of the music.

"For Lord's sake, Cassie—" Edward was replying, and neither one heard the other.

Sir Geoffrey took a deep breath, slackened his pace and made it appear as if he had strolled over, as if this were the most natural, casual thing in the world.

"Well, Edward! I say, Cassie, ain't this the thing, then? Only fancy runnin' into you here, Edward!"

It was the opening that could avoid any further demonstrations of a most unfortunate nature from either party, and Sir Geoffrey was hoping that they would take advantage of it. But Cassandra and Edward barely noticed him, so intent were they upon one another.

"I really fail to understand, madam wife, how you could present yourself in such a situation, in, I might add, such a condition! Have you no awareness of your position as a Duchess of Woodland?" Edward demanded in a steely voice.

Cassandra shrank back, but only for an instant. She knew that she was wrong, but that imp within her pushed her to stand her own ground. "And I might ask the same of you, sir! Do you feel your strawberry leaves entitle you to appear in this den of vice, like any 'prentice clerk out for an evening on the town?"

"It may not occur to you that I, as a man, may go to places where I would not care for my wife, as a female, to be seen!"

"So I have noticed! And in what company, I might add!"

"Pray do be seated, Sir Geoffrey! I fear we are to have one of those little domestic comedies our dramatists are so fond of putting upon the stage," Lady Chantry said, sotto voce, to the embarrassed dandy.

Acutely aware of the *maitre d's* eyes upon this tableau, Sir Geoffrey sat down. "Bad ton, oh, bad ton!" he muttered, in agony.

"Indeed, madam wife," Edward continued awfully, hating himself, yet unable to stop. "But my choice of company, you might remember, was in no way restricted by the bargain we made upon marriage!"

Cassandra bit her lip. Her head was swimming, and she was trembling with a fury that she could barely restrain. "If you had given the slightest thought to my feelings, instead of your own pleasures, Edward, perhaps you could have been more discreet in your relationships."

"If you had the faintest sense of maidenly propriety, Cassie, you wouldn't be here! What more did you want than to be a duchess? I gave you that, didn't I? Wasn't that what you wanted, to be able to flounce all over town with that train of mooncalves drooling all over your fan, Ardmore takin' you up in the Park? By God, Cassie, if you were a man, I swear I could call you out for your conduct!"

"And I would for yours, Edward! I know I am not beautiful or fascinating or in any way the sort of buxom cow upon which you set your heart, but—"

"Cassie!" Edward said horribly, and for a moment, she thought he would strike her, right there in front of everyone.

"Marriage à la mode," Lady Chantry said to Sir Geoffrey. It was plain she was enjoying this scene enormously. "I appeal to you, Sir Geoffrey. Am I a buxom cow?"

"Madam, you have done your damage," Sir Geoffrey replied automatically.

"Edward, I have tried so hard not to care—" Cassandra began miserably.

But he was not listening. "For Lord's sake, Cassie, let us say no more upon it now. Do you not see everyone looking at us?"

Edward had laid a restraining hand upon Cassandra's arm, but she wrenched free, turning to the lavender domino. "I appeal to you, Lady Chantry, please! You are very beautiful—everyone says so, and I am not, but Edward—"

With one gesture, Lady Chantry opened the silken cord on her mask and it fell away to reveal her face. The violet eyes glittered with amusement and something else, something that might have been triumph. "There you are, my dear. I am Lady Elizabeth Chantry, the buxom cow."

Cassandra flushed beneath her silk cover. The violet eyes held hers steadily, and then she surrendered, dropping her gaze to the delicate procelain snuffbox that lay upon the table. Almost against her will, Cassandra studied the delicate tracery, the outlines of satyrs and nymphs painted upon the cover. Something inside of her gave in defeat, and she raised her hands helplessly as if warding off an invisible blow.

"Your Grace, I believe the duchess is not feeling well." She heard Lady Chantry's voice, smooth and slow as honey, as if it came from far away.

Almost in a dream, she felt hands supporting her, watched Lady Chantry cover her face again with the mask, glimpsed Sir Geoffrey's distasteful posture, and Edward's tight-lipped fury. "Another one of Cassandra's knots—" someone was saying.

Edward's hands gripped her hard. "Geoff, will you see Lady Chantry home? I fear my wife is indisposed. Too much wine has gone to her head."

And he pushed Cassandra away, almost dragging her out the door into the cold night air, past the incurious stares of the Cyprians and the waiters and the linkboys, almost forcing her into the dark, cold sanctuary of their carriage.

Almost blindly, as if she were caught in a nightmare, Cassandra fell back against the squabs of the coach, finally wracked by tremors of fear and guilt. She felt rather than saw Edward seat himself beside her, ripping off his loo-mask in a single cold gesture, his thin profile sharply defined against the gaslights as the coach lurched down the street. His face was pale and tight with anger, the flesh drawn back from the bones, his eyes steel-blue as he looked straight ahead.

"Edward—" Cassandra began.

"We will discuss it tomorrow, if you please, madam wife." His voice was as cold as a rapier blade, and she instinctively knew if she pushed him further she would regret the consequences.

One large tear rolled down her cheek, and she dabbed at it with a corner of the wretched emerald domino, wishing herself dead, or at the very least back at the Gunnestons'.

In the morning, Cassandra rose from a sleepless bed. Like an automaton, she allowed Françoise to dress her hair and select a rather subdued morning dress of plain ivory cambric ornamented solely by a set of carved ivory buttons. Even Françoise's mercurial personality seemed subdued by the news that surely, Cassandra thought, staring blankly at her hollow-eyed image in the mirror, must be making the rounds of every morning call in London. Nervously, she shredded a lace handkerchief between her fingers, fighting back the tears.

Françoise had just fitted a lace cap over her mistress' curls when there was a knock on the door. Both women froze and their eyes met in the mirror; then Françoise turned to open the door.

Without waiting for her to do so, Edward strode into the room, still in his riding dress. If he too looked haggard and unhappy, Cassandra put it down to his controlled fury. Slowly, she turned from the dressing table to face him.

"You may leave us," he said to Françoise without taking his eyes from his wife. With one last protective look at her mistress, Françoise scurried away, closing the door behind her.

Cassandra's shoulders slumped, but Edward's cold gaze held her eyes as if he had hypnotized her, and she watched as he crossed the floor toward her dressing table, slapping his crop against his boot.

He stood towering above her for several long seconds before he spoke, and then his voice was cool and distant, as if he had carefully rehearsed his speech.

"When we entered into this farce of a marriage, Cassie, I genuinely believed that we could make a go of it, one way or another. I really felt that I had compromised you, but I also felt that you were old enough to know what your own mind was. All I can say is that I am very sorry things had to turn out the way they did for us. If you should wish to make application to divorce me, Cassie, I will provide you with such grounds as will leave you as little touched by scandal as possible."

"Divorce!" Cassandra exclaimed, feeling as if someone had clutched her heart in a cold hand. Divorce, for people like them, was almost unheard of. Couples would live apart, or live together in the most intense sort of misery, before they would consider such a shocking move. When one was married, it was forever, no matter what happened. Divorce was only undertaken in the most terrible circumstances, and as far as she knew, usually resulted in both parties becoming social outcasts. She was trembling, she realized suddenly, looking at her hand where the thin gold band glimmered faintly in the morning light.

"Of course, I am quite forgetting that you care very deeply for the pleasures of society, which I do not. Divorce would quite ruin that for you, would it not? But do not forget, you are a very wealthy woman, and it is possible to buy your way out such a trifle."

"As I have bought your mistress?" Cassandra flared, rising to her feet.

Edward's eyes narrowed to slits, but he did not flinch from the blow. "As I said, we entered into this contract knowing full well that my attentions, if not my affections, were engaged elsewhere. At the time, I was amused by your knowledge of this fact. But since you have attained the position of Duchess of Woodland, and you have all of the ton worshipping at your feet, I fail to see why you should figure me into your battle plan. Indeed, why you should betray jealousy at my connections baffles me, Cassie, for you seem to have quite a court of your own, any one of them ready to fulfill more—shall we say— adventuresome duties."

Slowly, Cassandra rose to her feet. While she did not quite come up to her husband's shoulder, she seemed to grow taller as she met his gaze with her own.

"To think—to think that I fancied that I loved you, Edward! When I recall how I clipped out your duty roster from the papers, how I prayed for your safe return, how I thought you were like a hero in some silly romantic novel—oh, I could laugh! Yes, *I* suggested the bargain. But I loved you, Edward. And I saw it as a way out of both our tangles! And my heart betrayed me last night."

Appalled at her own words, Cassandra sank down upon the stool again. A large tear coursed down her cheek, her eyes became red-rimmed, and her shoulders shook. "There!" she said in a muffled voice. "If you wish a divorce, you have all the reason in the world to seek one, for I married you under false pretenses, swearing there was no love. What did I know of love? It was a schoolgirl's tendre for a brave soldier, a hero." She lifted her face, made unattractive by tears, to his gaze. "And now, and now—I don't know what I feel, except, apparently, I have made a terrible mistake, all because I thought I loved you, and I wouldn't let her have you. Every time I turned around, every time it seemed as if we might be . . . close, *she* was there. Lord, what a jest!"

Edward stood gazing down at Cassandra, trying to sort out these tangled utterances, totally at a loss as to how to deal with her from there. That he had come to see her as much more than a milk-and-water schoolgirl, always in and out of scrapes, he found impossible to say; his pride would not allow such a thing. But he was stunned by her admission that she loved—*had* loved—him. It cast such an unexpected revelation upon her actions that he felt as if she had struck him. He was totally taken aback, and for once in his life did not know how to proceed.

Stunned, he turned on his heel and left the room. Cassandra stared miserably at the closed door, wishing herself dead.

After this interview, affairs between the duke and the duchess continued on in an even more remote ambiance than before, if possible. If both were slightly subdued, and more discreet in their conduct, neither one made the slightest attempt to communicate further with the other. The word "divorce" hung between them like a two-edged sword.

Only one of the four parties at that disastrous evening in Covent Garden had any reason to wish to spread word of that encounter any further. While Sir Geoffrey would deny the entire thing, and no one would think to question either Edward or Cassandra, Lady Chantry's tongue was sharp, and her acquaintance notorious among certain gentlemen.

Therefore, the scandal, much enlarged and embroidered upon with each telling, soon made its rounds through the ton. And if there were those who would dismiss it as backstairs gossip, not fit to be repeated, there were others, less charitable, who were delighted to pass the story on, taking as much pleasure from their own speculations as from the bare bones of the tale.

Cassandra held her head up in public, and was still to be seen driving her phaeton and four in the park with any one of a number of admirers, or standing up for the waltz at any of a number of balls and parties about town. For his part, Edward continued on in much the same way he had before with the exception of a notable absence from Half-Moon Street, but even their most staunch defenders could not help but notice a distinct coolness between the couple.

And if this rumor was duly celebrated in the gossip columns of the day, both duke and duchess were able to shrug it off as a matter of total indifference. But privately, both could admit, however independently, to their mutual and very unhappy cousin Sir Geoffrey Russell-Broome, that it was a very unpleasant experience to have all the world know of one's most intimate affairs. It seemed, both said sadly, only a matter of time before the duchess would file her petition with the House of Lords. There seemed to be no other way out of this latest Cassandra knot.

The letter, when it came, was addressed to both the duke and the duchess. Kellog, recognizing the Dowager's strong handwriting, cast up his eyebrows as if petitioning a higher power for some help in this quarter, delivered the missive to Her Grace.

Whatever the dowager said, it was sufficient for Cassandra to throw open her door and demand of the departing Kellog that he summon the duke to her boudoir at once.

Feeling much more hopeful than he had for some months, Kellog picked up his step and delivered the message to His Grace's man. Both would have been less than human had they not exchanged a hopeful glance. In their long years of service with the Talbot household, they had never known the Dowager's power to fail, whether she was putting off the bailiff or patching up a romance.

Cautiously, Edward made his appearance in Cassandra's writing room. She was seated at her desk, turning the document in question over in her hand, an unfathomable look upon her face.

Without comment, she turned the letter over to her spouse, and as he skimmed through the familiar handwriting, she sat quietly staring out the window, across the gray park in the square where nursemaids supervised their charges' airings.

When at last he had finished, he swore softly under his breath. "So, she says she is ill—" he murmured, his voice trailing away.

Cassandra nodded. "She wishes us to come to Woodland Manor as soon as possible."

"I've never known her to have a bad day's health in her life!" Edward's voice was slightly shaken.

"It cannot be as bad as all that. Surely, it must be influenza, or some other trivial malady that she will emerge from, feeling right as trivet within a few days," Cassandra suggested hopefully. "Oh, Edward, I cannot see Godmamma—" She broke off.

Edward's jaw tightened. "Let us hope that you're right, Cassie. How soon may you be ready to go into Devon?"

"I can be packed in a trice. Should you want to put the

coachman round immediately? I do not think we should wait."

"A half-hour's time, Cassie. I do not feel that we should linger. Kellog may make our excuses. Good God! Grand'mère! One always pictured the old lady to be immortal."

It was clear that he was shaken. Cassandra, forgetting their quarrel, grasped his hand in her own and felt the returning pressure. "Oh, I hope it may not be serious!" she said quietly. "Edward, what are we to do?"

"The only thing we can, under these circumstances, Cassie. We must go directly to her."

CHAPTER 9

WITH some final hastily given orders to Kellog, Edward threw Cassandra up into the squabs of his curricle and seized the reins from his groom. He brought the team about, and they rumbled down the cobblestones of Grosvenor Square.

Edward threaded his way through the ponderous London traffic at breakneck speed, passing the Dover Mail with only inches to spare, narrowly avoiding a nightsoil cart and taking the South Gate well ahead of a landauet.

Cassandra pressed her hands firmly over her bonnet and closed her eyes as His Grace overtook a dray moving stolidly toward the Tower Underpass. She bit back an unpleasant remark on Edward's driving abilities, and her heart twisted as she thought of the Dowager. If it was not for her concern, she would have demanded to be set down at the Green Man, very conveniently forgetting her own admiration of the duke's notable skills as a whip.

Leaving Lincoln's Field Inn behind, Edward was able to maintain his team at a steady pace, barely turning the ribbons in his hands as he took a sharp curve in the road on two wheels, pulling out into the long open stretch that announced the beginning of the Great Plymouth Road.

As they sailed past the snug prosperous farms and the small country inns nestled into the brown winter landscape, cold wind began to slap at Cassandra's face. She wished she had allowed herself to dress with more concern for warmth than style.

With cold tears in her eyes, she buried her hands deeper into her ermine muff, pulled the beaver lap robe more tightly about her legs, bracing herself against the ruts in the road.

Edward spoke to her only once, to demand in a voice as chill as the weather if she were warm enough in that rig.

"Quite comfortable!" Cassandra replied primly, though the wind stung at her cheeks as she felt as if her feet were in danger of frostbite. She would rather have frozen to death than admit discomfort.

At the Pelican and Feather of Salisbury, Edward changed his team, and Cassandra took advantage of the brief stopover to procure a hot brick for her feet. The few minutes they spent alone in the parlor reserved for the quality were uncomfortably silent. Both were relieved when the landlord called the change and they could proceed on their way. On the open road there was less time to think of themselves or the plight of the Dowager, who, Cassandra believed, must even now be lying at death's door.

With only one more change of horses at Honiton, they proceeded without mishap, each wrapped in a haughty silence.

The sun was sinking low across the hills when they turned through Ottery St. Mary's into the narrow country lane that led to the sea and the village of Woodland Green.

Not even the most charitable guidebook could call Woodland Manor an elegant ducal seat. A Saxon fortress against invaders from the sea had been roughly translated into a Plantagenet castle, and such parts of it as had been torn down and added upon by succeeding generations of Talbots finally resembled nothing so much as an architect's nightmare. The Plantagenet cloister had been buttressed by a Tudor wing, and a Sheridan telescope was brought up, shifted by a Palladian conservatory and flanked by a pseudo-Romanesque portico of unmistakable ugliness. The entire effect was unfortunately further offset by several generations of penurial neglect with the results that only the more modern wings were fit for habitation, and the main structure had fallen into an ivy-covered decay strongly suggestive of the more Gothic novels of Mrs. Radcliffe. To those who knew Woodland Manor, it was not without a certain charm, but strangers had been known to enter only with the greatest trepidations.

"Ho! Dauntle!" Edward cried as they swept under the portico and he reined in the team. He peered about for the Dowager's ancient butler, whose invariable habit it had been to greet him as soon as his wheels were heard in the drive.

But the huge oaken door was moved only a few inches back on its hinges, to reveal a brief glimpse of a pale face before closing again.

Edward swung himself down from the seat and pulled on the bell-rope. The ancient iron clarion echoed within the great stone hall, and the door slowly opened again.

" 'Old on, 'old on! It takes a mort o'muscle to open this 'ere great glammoring portal, it does!" cried a strange voice, pushing the door back with the greatest effort to reveal himself in the fading light as a complete stranger. He looked Edward, then Cassandra, up and down for several seconds, then nodded his head. "Thought so. You must be the duke and duchess wot the flash mort—the Dowager is expectin'. Step right in, an' I'll fetch round the stableman for your cattle, if you please."

The Duke of Woodland could raise his brows questioningly at this astounding individual without causing him the least discomfort; he assisted Cassandra down from her perch and took up her portmanteau under his arm, turning on his heel to lead them back into the hall.

Well below the medium height, this remarkable individual looked like anything but a butler. His dark, thin hair grew down his long, thin face in a widow's peak, and his eyebrows rose up to meet it in a natural expression of surprise. A pair of darting black eyes seemed to miss nothing except the long, thin nose placed between them. He resembled nothing so much as a singularly intelligent fox, Cassandra decided, and her initial impression was confirmed by his stealthy, vulpine movements as he crossed the echoing empty stone hall.

"I say, my good man, where is Dauntle?" Edward demanded suspiciously, his hand moving to the inner pocket of his great coat where he kept his traveling arm, a small single shot pistol.

" 'Ar, the old one's daughter did need 'is attentions in 'Oniton. Seems as if she's been confined with her sixth cub, and 'Er Grace sent 'im off to look after the master's pub, the place bein' so busy. So, 'Er Grace took me on, temporary like, until 'e's gamming back. 'Er Grace is in the writing room, makin' up the lists for the party. She allowed as 'ow you was to be sent on up, Duke—pardon, Your Grace. I'm a bit raw to this butler-lay, ma'am," he confided to Cassandra, stepping aside to allow her to pass.

"Her Grace is planning a party?" Edward demanded.

The vulpine person shrugged in his ill-fitting livery. " 'At's what she told me after lunch. Said she wasn't to be disturbed, something about seating arrangements needin' some concentration."

Cassandra grasped Edward's arm. "It must be brain fever!" she whispered, her eyes wide. "Poor Godmamma must have sunk quite low to allow this man to serve in Dauntle's stead!"

"We shall go up to the Dowager at once," Edward said, thrusting his hat and cape at the surprised servant. "There is no need to announce us."

He hurried Cassandra through the drafty stone passageway up the stairs. "She must be in her dotage to be hiring a jailbird. The writing room! Good God, what next?"

"I wonder if Strawbridge has had the forethought to call a doctor? Your grandmother ought not to be out of bed, wandering about the house in a fever—" Cassandra murmured breathlessly. "Oh, I hope we are not too late!"

Fully expecting to find the Dowager trembling with fever and half-mad with delirious ramblings, Edward and Cassandra burst into the small pleasant study the Dowager maintained beside her bedchamber.

"Cassandra! Edward! My dearest loves! I did not expect you until quite late this evening!" Looking as fine as a fivepence, and very becoming in an ivory dress and cap, the Dowager rose from her desk and extended two firm hands to her children, presenting a very rosy cheek for a kiss. "Indeed, I thought perhaps you would stay overnight at Honiton! I shall immediately send down to Cook to put up the veal rack, and send Grubb up with the tea tray, for you must be quite chilled to the bone—"

"Grand'mère!" Edward said in oppressively quiet tones, which boded ill for his parent. "Pray what does this mean?"

Cassandra clutched her godmother's hands and searched her face anxiously for signs of senile dementia, but the twinkle in that lady's blue eyes assured her that she was in full possession of her faculties. "G-God-mamma, you wrote to us and said that you were upon your deathbed, imploring us to come before it was too late!"

To her credit, the Dowager had the grace to blush very faintly, but she soon made a recovery, kissing her god-daughter's cheek. She beamed merrily upon them both, shaking her head slightly. "Did I say that? I did not precisely mean to give the impression that I had decided to stick my spoon in the wall just yet! 'Pon rep, I was feeling a slight bit under the weather and a trifle lonely, I suppose, and I may have exaggerated just a very tiny bit, but how nice it is to have you here! An old woman, living alone in the country, does get so lonely for her children at times, you know. So, I was just arranging the seating for the small country dance I planned in your honor tomorrow night—" With a spritely step, she crossed the carpet and pulled on the bell cord. "Only a few of our closest and oldest friends in the neighborhood, to introduce Cassandra as our new duchess, Edward, so do not look daggers at me in that fashion. Now you will have some nice tea and some of the little cakes you are so fond of, and you may rest a while before dinner."

Edward and Cassandra exchanged a look. Edward's jaw worked most unpleasantly, but he contented himself with throwing his gloves upon the table in a very forceful manner.

Cassandra allowed the Dowager to undo the strings of Cassandra's bonnet and lead her to a chair by the fire where she could warm her frozen hands. Edward asked, "Grand'mère, might one ask who that person was who admitted us? And what have you done with Dauntle?"

The Dowager chafed Cassandra's cold hands. "Oh, Grubb. Yes, I suppose he is a trifle unusual, is he not?" She chuckled. "But he is very clever, I think, and his colorful, ah, attitude certainly amuses me."

"He looks like a fox!" Edward said, hands on hips, glaring down at his grandmother suspiciously. "And what's more, if he's a butler, I'm the King of Spain!"

"Yes, he does bear a rather interesting resemblance to an animal, does he not? He tells me it runs in his father's family, and that he had an uncle who ran a tea shop in Bath who was universally known as Foxy!"

"I'd lay a monkey he's a jailbird! Outside of enough, my dear!"

"Edward, you will not address your grandmother in such tones, if you please. You will remember that I could take a hairbrush to the seat of your pants!"

"Oh, Lord!" Edward sighed, throwing his hands up in despair. "I surrender!" He tossed himself into a chair and stretched his long legs out to the fire.

The Dowager nodded with satisfaction. "Very well, Edward, you must learn not to *stew,* or you will go off precisely like your great-grandfather, with a terrible fit of apoplexy. I assure you that Grubb comes to me on the highest recommendation, and that he is not a jailbird, as you put it."

She settled her skirts into the small chaise and beamed upon them both. "Now, you must tell me precisely what all the latest crim-cons and on-dits of Town are! I understand the Duchess of Devonshire—the new one—has borne yet another brat, and this one within wedlock. A most amazing household!"

Since Edward and Cassandra were the source of the latest on-dit, they could not bring themselves to formulate a reply to the Dowager's query, but it dawned upon them both that the reasons they had been summoned so urgently into the country had nothing to do with the Dowager's health, and a great deal to do with their own conduct, for despite her protestations to the contrary, the

Dowager was always quite well-informed on all the London gossip.

Fortunately, at that moment, Grubb chose to appear with the tea tray. Cassandra watched in fascination as he awkwardly bore the overloaded silver tray through the door and into the room, his soft slippers padding almost stealthily across the floor, his vulpine face set in a determined, almost theatrical mask of butlerishness. She suddenly wondered if he had learned his trade from plays. She held her breath, watching the saucers and cups teetering precariously over the petits-fours as he lay the tray on the table before the Dowager.

"Right jolly mort what's fryin' up the dinner," he whispered to the Dowager. "Friday-faced female threatened to take me nose off with a meat cleaver if I didn't stop paul-prying into the doings of 'er brothers."

"Cook has been here for years upon years, Grubb," the Dowager replied evenly, pouring out the tea. "She has a memory like a trap, and doesn't miss a thing. But you should not ask about her brothers, for they are generally supposed to be about the free-trading business."

"Hist!" Grubb whistled, nodding wisely at his mistress. "Don't that explain it all, though! Well, I thank ye, Duchess, for now I shall know just 'ow to be treadin' in that quarter!" Recovering himself, he sketched a conspiratorial bow. "Will ye be needin' anything else, Your Grace?"

"Just ask Cook to set out the veal rack. And keep your—what was your expression—your *oggles fastened on about the house!*"

Grubb nodded and made his stealthy exit, closing the door behind himself with elaborate gentility.

"Grand'mère!" Edward exclaimed as soon as he judged Grubb to be out of earshot. "What in heaven's name are you and that—that Grubb doing? 'Keeping your oggles fastened on' cant!"

The Dowager thrust a steaming cup of Lapsang Souchong into his hands. "Nothing, I assure you, my love, that you need concern yourself with. I find Grubb to be a most interesting individual with so many interesting expressions."

"Inland Revenue!" Cassandra said. "Oh, Godmamma, pray be careful! If anything were to happen to you—"

"Inland Revenue? And what would I be doing with a customs man in the house, when you know perfectly well that we have always turned a blind eye to the kegs of brandy stored in the chapel? Why, our own cellars are stocked from the Gentlemen! I am surprised at you! Absolutely surprised!"

"But to have a gallowsman as your butler! Grand'mère, that is outside of enough!"

The Dowager shook her head mysteriously. "Grubb is no gallowsbird, I assure you," she said firmly. "Now, as I was saying, I do sometimes manage to hear just the barest scraps of gossip from Town. My dear friend Lady Ombersley, such a good correspondent, with such a fine eye for these things—" She passed Cassandra a plate of cakes. "Yes, my dear, you must have at least one to keep up your strength after your journey. You may imagine how very distressing I found it when Sophia Ombersley reported—very reluctantly—that you—the pair of you have been acting in a very odd manner. The word 'divorce' has been bandied about in connection with your names."

Cassandra flushed and looked at her feet. She noted that the stitching in one of her boots was coming undone. From a great distance away, she heard Edward's drawling voice.

"Have we been lured here on false pretenses, then?" Edward demanded. "First you tell us that you're at death's door, then you spring a lecture upon us! Doin' it a bit too brown, ma'am, when all the world knows that you and Grandfather were frequently at odds."

"The word 'divorce,' Godmamma, is perhaps too hard. Surely you cannot be influenced by idle and destructive gossip," Cassandra said, placing her hand on the other woman's arm. The Dowager patted Cassandra reassuringly, but her tone was severe.

With a great dignity, the Dowager sipped at her tea. "Since we are all among the family, I feel that we may speak frankly. Edward, the word was never breathed between your grandfather and me. Of course we had our disagreements. What married couple does not? And one could certainly not have called our marriage a love match, such as is so fashionable nowadays. But you must admit that the pair of you have become a topic of conversation in such a way as to cause a great deal of anxiety to one who is concerned for your mutual happiness. My dear children, your grandfather and I contrived to settle our differences in an atmosphere of tolerance and discretion that you would do well to consider!"

"Grand'mère—"

"No, I shall have my say, if you please, Edward! The pair of you have contrived to remain friends, since Cassandra was in leading strings, and I fail to see why your relationship should be thus cast over by a few words and a piece of paper."

"Since that excessively odd person downstairs refused to show me up, I suppose I shall have to announce myself!" exclaimed a merry voice in the threshold. "Lady Julia Talbot at your service!"

Impervious to the baleful stares cast in her direction, a very tall young girl in a modest pelisse and a far too dashing bonnet burst upon the scene. She bore a marked resemblance to Edward, with the same long narrow face and dark hair, but her gray eyes betrayed a certain sense of humor alien to her elder brother's countenance. "Grand'mère, Edward, Cassie, my love, we are now sisters! Is that not famous? Your butler came down to inform me that you had left for Devon in a great hurry. I would have been left standing on the doorstep, I believe, if Geoffrey had not come along precisely at that moment, but I knew that it was all a hum about Grand'-mère being sick, because she never is." As she spoke, Lady Julia moved about the room, bestowing hearty embraces upon each of her relations. "Is it not famous? The last thing I expected was that Miss Rumboldt would catch the measles, and, of course, since I have not had them, Mary Fraser and India Mapstone and Lydia Stanton-Yonge and I were all sent down early. So, Lord Stanton-Yonge took us all to London in his coach, which is quite the thing, with his crest on the door and purple squabs, and I went about to your house, but you had left, and I should probably have had to stay at the Stanton-Yonges' until Willie, you remember Willie, he had spots, only he does not anymore, and in fact is quite dashing in his Hussar uniform, went to Waiter's or someplace to find Geoff, except at that moment Geoff came up the walkway, and asked where I got this bonnet, which I think is very fetching, even if Miss Rumboldt does not, and, oh, Cassie, thank you so much for the silk stockings, they were exactly what I wanted, and the lawn caps are very nice, and of course Geoff did not want to rusticate at all, but I persuaded him that if I did not, I would be stranded in London and he would have to take Lydia and me to Astley's Amphitheatre, which he did not want to do, so off we came, just like the wind, in a post chaise!" She paused for breath and smiled sunnily around at the company.

"Good Lord," Edward said, sorting out this tangled speech. "Not only am I saddled with you but Geoff also? This is outside of enough!"

"Miss Rumboldt could not have chosen a more unfortunate time in which to catch the measles!" The Dowager said bitterly. "Of course, my darling, I am always glad to have you with me, but really, that woman could not have chosen a more unfortunate time in which to be ill!"

Lady Julia, blissfully ignorant of the storm brewing about her head, seized her sister-in-law and held her at arm's length, inspecting her cornsilk-gold merino traveling dress. "How good you look, Cassie! Why, one would have been pressed to recognize you in your transformation! Geoff has been telling me every single detail of your miraculous transformation. D'you suppose he will do the same for me upon my come-out? And now everyone calls you the Original! It's outside of fantasy! When you present me, will I have as much ton? If I am to make a push,

Geoff says that I will have to do something terribly outrageous, such as dipping snuff or riding astride!"

"Good Lord, Grand'mère, do I have to endure this minx as well?" Edward complained under his breath.

Julia paused in her minute examination of the underpinnings of Cassandra's hairstyle and flashed her unsympathetic brother a missish grin. "Oh, pray stop frowning at me in that odious way, Edward, as if I had fetched a runner! It can hardly be termed my fault that Miss Rumboldt came down with the measles! You look as if I had planned this!" She seized Cassandra's fingers in her own. "You must be called upon to defend me from my dragonish brother now, my love. Tell me, do you allow him to ride roughshod all over you? You must not, you know!"

"Oh dear, two more covers for dinner. I shall simply have to add another set to the country dances, then," the Dowager said vaguely, throwing up her hands in despair of ever attaining a set-down for her errant children.

"Aunt Augusta, that man is a dashed loose screw! Calls himself a butler and tries to take m'beaver between his fingers" Do I look as if I want fingermarks on my hat?" Sir Geoffrey, resplendent in a buff driving coat with no less than sixteen capes, huffed into the room. "Servant, Edward, Cassie! All very well for you to laugh, but that great lout didn't attempt to destroy your best hat with his greasy fingerprints. Aunt Augusta, what noddle have you got in your cockloft to engage such a person?"

"She won't tell you," Edward said ominously. "All we have been able to determine is that he is not with Inland Revenue."

"I should hope not. Been dealin' with the Gentlemen myself anytime these past ten years. Dashed if I want a great lot of taxes on my brandy. Well, Aunt, I've delivered your gel to you, safe and sound, though why Julia had to pick on me, I have no idea. Bad ton to be seen with a schoolroom miss in a bonnet like that! Why, people might think I was hanging out in the petticoat line. Quite ruin my reputation if it got about that a cousin of mine was clappin' such a piece of foolishness on her head, don't you know."

Julia giggled. "One would never know just how fond you are of me, Geoffrey, to hear you talk that way. I think it's very fetching!" But she removed the offending headgear.

"When I was a girl, feathers and flowers together were considered quite *fast*," the Dowager remarked thoughtfully.

Edward regarded his relations with mounting disgust. "What a madhouse!" he cried at last, stalking out of the room in search of brandy.

"Whatever did you do, Cassandra, to be saddled with such a groating bore as my brother? I declare, Edward has become quite odious in his dotage!"

Cassandra turned large green eyes upon Julia. She could only press her hand against the other girl's as her emotions threatened to overcome her. With a strangled apology, she turned and fled the room, overcome with tears.

Julia stared at the closed door in astonishment, then turned a puzzled face to her grandmother. "Whatever did I say?" she demanded, genuinely puzzled. "No one could be more pleased than I that Edward has finally recognized what we have all known for ages, that Cassie has been head over heels in love with him anytime these past ten years and more—oh! Did I say something terribly dreadful?"

Sir Geoffrey cleared his throat and focused his attention upon an invisible speck of lint on his lapel.

"Yes," the Dowager finally replied, folding her list.

Lady Julia shook her dark head. "Not that odious woman again! Oh, no!"

"It would do well to keep a civil tongue in your head, miss!" Sir Geoffrey commented drily. "Dashed bad of you to go about teasing your grandmother for things you ain't even supposed to know about."

"Everyone knows!" Julia retorted. "Bath is not that far from London!"

"Oh, both of you, stop your bickering!" the Dowager exclaimed. "Nothing could have gone more far afield than this day! Now I must think!"

Lady Julia and Sir Geoffrey looked at the Dowager as if she had suddenly taken leave of her senses. The elder duchess sat up in her chair and closed her eyes, a slight frown creasing her brow, meditating upon what fresh scheme she could devise. She was, as many could testify, a female of inexhaustible resource, perpetual optimism, and iron will. "My dears," she sighed at last, "you have thrown my plans for reconciling Edward and Cassandra totally awry, and it has taken me two weeks to hit upon this particular ploy of inducing them to come into the country and away from town life's snares. I shall simply have to think again."

Gently, Sir Geoffrey led Lady Julia, still carrying her offending bonnet in her hand, from the room. "Hard work, thinkin'," he remarked sympathetically.

Several hours later, Lady Julia, looking more demure in the pink and white sprigged muslin her grandmother deemed suitable for a young female not yet out, knocked upon Cassandra's door. Without bothering to wait for a reply, she walked into the room.

Cassandra was sitting at the dressing table in a dinner dress of ivory peau-de-soie, her eyes hollow and clouded as she stared with unseeing eyes at Strawbridge's work upon her hairstyle.

Edward, already in his evening dress, stood with his arms folded across his chest, staring down at his wife. "—could find some way of reaching an agreement, Madam. Oh, Cassie—" he was saying, raising his hands imploringly. "Good Lord, Julia, didn't they teach you to knock, at Miss Rumboldt's?" he demanded angrily, confronting his sister.

Julia shook her head and shrugged, taking in the agitated manner in which Cassandra was twisting a spangled scarf of celestial blue through her fingers, and heedless of the pleading expression on Cassandra's face. "I've come for a cose with my sister-in-law, Edward. Why don't you run along and keep Geoff company, instead of browbeating poor Cassie. Really, I'd think that you'd already done your damage for one day, Edward." She sniffed. "The last time I saw Geoff, he was casting a fit because Grubb had managed to leave a spot on one of the neckcloths he'd sent for pressing."

"Cassandra, we will continue this discussion later," Edward said drily. With a short, ironic bow at his sister, he left the room just as Cassandra rose from the dressing table to reach out to him.

The door closed behind him. Cassandra dabbed at her eyes with the spangled scarf, then threw it down on the dressing table. "Oh, damn and *double damn!*" she moaned in a tight voice, pressing her hands against her flaming cheeks.

Julia slipped an arm about Cassandra's shoulders. "There, there, Cassie. Grand'mère says that all newly-weds have some problems adjusting. I daresay when I marry, I shall drive my poor husband out of his mind, unless he is extremely indulgent, which will probably be very doubtful, since I don't believe I could stand an indulgent husband."

Cassandra blew her nose into her handkerchief. "It's all my fault!" she gasped. "If only I could keep a still tongue in my head! Oh, Julia, if you only knew just how bad things were, you would not make so light of it! Marriage is a trap!"

"I suppose I wouldn't know, but you know what black moods Edward can get into when everything is not precisely the way he likes it to be. What a lovely scarf! Do look, Cassie, is it not exactly the color of my eyes?"

Seeking a way to divert her sister-in-law, Julia picked up the glittering rectangle and held it against her face. "How much better it will be when I do not have to wear this pastel! Come, my love, cheer up! Doubtless he will have forgotten the whole affair by dinner time. Edward always calms down, if you allow him some time to collect what a cake he is making of himself! Come now, let us go downstairs! There is a full moon tonight, and it looks so beautiful, out against the cove!"

Reluctantly Cassandra rose from the stool and allowed the younger woman to fuss at the curls Strawbridge had so carefully dressed not an hour before. Arm in arm, the two women started down the steps.

"Oh! My reticule!" Julia exclaimed, almost stamping her foot. "I left it in your room! Do you go on down and I'll run back and fetch it up!"

Despite Julia's prediction, Cassandra found only Sir Geoffrey in the drawing room, sitting upon the settee, gazing out across the moonlit lawns toward the magnificent sweep of the ocean. He started as she entered the room and threw her a murderous look. It was clear that his ill mood of the afternoon had yet to abate.

"Cassie!" he cried. "By God, gal, you startled me!"

Cassandra muttered a lethargic apology, and sank listlessly into a wing chair by the fireplace. "Poor Geoff," she sighed, "it seems a great deal too bad that you should also be dragged into this Cheltenham tragedy."

Sir Geoffrey shrugged politely. "Needed to rusticate m'self anyway. Town rather thin of company, holiday season and all that. No family to speak of, rather depressing to linger at one's club. Good thing to rusticate for a day or two."

"Nonetheless, it cannot help but be a dead bore for you to have to endure yet another bout of the—differences between Edward and myself."

Sir Geoffrey found himself preoccupied by the storm clouds rolling in across the ocean. By morning, they would be fogged in, he ventured to say. Such was the danger of living near the seaside, not to mention the way the unhealthy damp could creep through the old house. Doubtless by morning, he would feel quite crippled up with the ague. He always did at Woodland Manor.

Cassandra picked at the lace on her dress and said nothing. She had always loved Woodland Manor for its wild, romantic proximity to the coast.

Julia fluttered into the room, dangling her reticule over her arm. "Gracious, what a night it is to be! I have just been talking to that very strange butler—Grunge? Grubb! What an excessively odd little man. Grand'mère's penchant for surrounding herself with characters is quite out of the ordinary, is it not? He was telling me the strangest tale! Someone broke into Sophia Ombersley's house and stole that great enormous diamond of hers! He says that it's the seventh or eighth such theft in five years! He says that the burglar never strikes in any pattern, but he always preys upon ladies of the highest ton, and he always seems to know exactly where to look for the jewels!"

At that tidbit of Town gossip, Sir Geoffrey's spirits seemed to perk up a bit.

"What! Someone stole Sophie's Star of Bombay! Doesn't that beat the band! Seems to me that about this time last year, or was it the year before, everyone was talking about how Lady Carnett's famous rubies were purloined. She'd come in and left them in the case on the dressing table, and the next morning when her abigail came to put them away in the safe, they were gone, case and all. Lord, what a hum there was about that!" He shook his head. "They'd been in the Carnett family for years and years, and old Carnett was quite put out about it; gave her a terrible set-down for being so careless!"

"Grubb says that in his opinion, it's the work of the same person, and that the jewels are taken to Holland and cut up and sold. He says that whoever the burglar is, he knows exactly where to look! He must crawl in through the window!" Julia shivered with delight.

"Aunt Gunneston had a friend who lost a set of diamonds and sapphires in just such a way—" Cassandra said vaguely. Prodded into giving the details, she shrugged reluctantly. "She was in the habit of concealing them in the pocket of an old pelisse in her wardrobe, rather than keeping them in the lock box. Apparently, she believed that would be the last place a thief would look. But they went away to Switzerland for her health, and someone broke into the house and knew *exactly* where to look. And of course, the house was closed up, so they did not discover the theft until they returned, but she was quite prostrate with anger, and took to her bed for a week."

"Old Lady Thraston! A more Friday-faced, pious old hypocrite I would not be able to find!" Sir Geoffrey remarked idly. "Served her right, at least."

"Grubb says that one would be amazed if one knew how many females stuff their jewels in a drawer in the dressing table or toss their baubles on the bureau when they come in from a ball or a party! He says that ladies of the ton can be especially careless when it comes to leaving things strewn about, and that a very clever burglar has little trouble gaining entrance to some of the very best mansions in the city!"

"Quite so," Sir Geoffrey muttered. "I say though, Jule, you shouldn't be gossiping with the butler. Fellow looks as if he might be the burglar himself!"

Julia shrugged. "Oh, but he knows everyone! Imagine, he saw Peyser, the Lincoln Fields Inn Highwayman, hanged at Tyburn."

"That will do, Lady Julia!" Edward said briskly as he walked into the room. With a short, restrained bow at Cassandra and a nod to Geoffrey, he helped himself to a glass of canary and stood by the window. It was abundantly clear that he was still in his black mood. "It may be right and clear for your grandmother to employ whoever she sees fit, but I forbid you to go about repeating low tales."

"Well!" Julia cried, but the look she was served by her brother was so dark that she lapsed into silence, satisfying herself with a sulky face.

"Edward, please!" Cassandra begged him. "Julia was simply telling us that Sophia Ombersley has had her Star of Bombay stolen."

The duke turned to look down at his wife. His expression was not pleasant. "Will you now attempt to tell me how I must conduct my dealings with my sister, madam wife? I do not feel that your conduct is sufficiently above reproach to allow you to guide my actions!"

Cassandra, stung, flushed to the roots of her hair. "And what of yours, sir? I fail to see how you could sustain!" she exclaimed in a rare burst of spirit.

Edward smiled thinly. The cold eyes that bore down upon Cassandra made her flinch beneath his gaze. "There are times, Cassie, when I could wish you in Hell," he said evenly. "You may feel that your fortune gives you leave to speak as you please, but the truth is far from that!"

Cassandra could only stare at Edward, unable to formulate a reply. A shocked silence, louder than noise, had fallen over the company. Sir Geoffrey attempted to become invisible, while Julia stared from one to the other, her pale expression betraying her distress at this unexpected glimpse of the uglier side of domestic discord.

Slowly, Cassandra rose to her feet. "If this is the way it shall be then perhaps we are better separated! I—I wish I had never married you! I wish you had died at Waterloo! I wish I could—"

"Kill me? Yes, wouldn't you like to?" Edward replied.

"Your fortunes did not buy you a complaisant husband, madam wife," he continued, "as much as you might have wished that they would. Perhaps you would have been better off casting those missish airs off long ago and revealing yourself for what you are—a harebrained flirt, a schoolgirl still pulling herself in and out of scrapes! By God, Cassie, if you were a man, I should have—"

"Beggin' your pardon, sir," Grubb's voice drawled across Edward's speech, and he spun to stare at the small man, standing in the doorway, his vulpine eyes taking in everything, his ill-fitting livery streaked with flour on the sleeve. "Ah, dinner is served," Grubb concluded, meeting the duke's eyes squarely.

Julia gave a false, twittering laugh. "Yes, let us go in and eat. Perhaps a full stomach will quench some of your anger, Edward."

"Let us hope," Sir Geoffrey muttered below his breath. "Bad ton, don't you know, dashed bad ton to be goin' at your wife in the library before dinner. Likely to put your guests off their feed, don't you know?"

The Dowager seemed to have put off the course of action for Edward and Cassandra. At dinner she seemed to be wholly occupied with the peccadilloes of her cook, a mistress of culinary skill with uncertain temperament, who, upon discovering that her carefully planned menu of oyster pie, beef pudding, asparagus Hélène and *pomme confiture,* together with nine or ten lesser removes, was being returned to her kitchen barely touched, had thrown a spatula at the scullery maid and produced what the Dowager could term only a very indifferent roulade. Fortunately, Master Edward was a particular favorite of hers, and she outdid herself to produce a magnificent raspberry syllabub.

Julia's high-strung volubility more than made compensation for the singlar lack of conversation about the board's other diners. Seated opposite one another, Edward drank more than he ate, and Cassandra, her eyes downcast, only picked indifferently at her plate.

Sir Geoffrey's sense of propriety was too nice to allow him to fall into the silence of his cousins, and he made a credible effort to maintain an even flow of conversation with Julia and the Dowager, but his discomfort, usually so easily conquered, was thrown over by Grubb's wholly inept service at table. And, dash it, the man was positively staring at him throughout the meal.

"Wine served to the right, removed to the left!" he finally took upon himself to hiss at the butler, flapping his napkin in that menial's direction.

After what seemed to be an eternity to Sir Geoffrey, the meal was finally finished and the covers removed.

The ladies withdrew to the drawing room, the Dowager announcing that she hoped they would not keep her waiting too long as she wanted a rubber of piquet before retiring.

Edward glowered at Sir Geoffrey as he lit his cigarillo, and that gentleman resigned himself for once and all to a long and unpleasant stay at Woodland Manor. He was no stranger to his cousin's black moods.

Accordingly, he settled down in his chair and watched with mounting horror as Grubb served the port. "I say, m'good man, you don't decant port!" Sir Geoffrey protested as the crystal bottle was placed upon the table. "Sacrilege to decant port!"

Grubb looked down at the offending bottle placidly. "Forgive, sir! Bein' as how I'm not accustomed to the ways of the swells, and Her Grace tellin' me to put the sherry into one o' them cut-glass bottles—"

"We'll drink it," Edward cut him short. "You may go. Take your fiver-face elsewhere, if you please!"

Grubb's narrow face lit up and his lips twitched. "Ar, Your Grace, 'ow'd you know I'd been in the ring?"

"Up to your weight? I say it's that smashed-up ear of yours. Bantamweight?"

Grubb nodded. "Fought the Turkish Wonder, I did. Ten stone match. And a rare mill it were, Your Grace. Not what you might be used to at Jackson's." He turned on his heel and left the room, a sardonic grin across his features.

Edward shook his head. "The Turkish Wonder. The Turkish Wonder—small sort of man from Birmingham, as I collect, but when would Grubb have boxed with the Turkish Wonder? He was sent to Botany Bay for his involvement in a false stock speculation—" For a second, Edward's face betrayed a sense of satisfaction, as if he had put a particularly annoying piece of a puzzle together.

"Stock fraud? Not the counterfeiting thing at the exchange, five, six years ago?" Sir Geoffrey asked.

Edward shrugged. "Perhaps so. I can't recall the details. Only read about it in the papers from home. I was in Spain then." He drew his eyebrows together and poured the port into the glasses with a slightly unsteady hand.

"Geoff, it's the deuces to pay with Cassandra!" he said darkly. "And now m'grandmother's got some bee in her cap that she can bring it all about again. But that, my coz, is something that would tax the powers of Job! I think—between you and me, coz!—that the only solution is to become unbuckled! Best thing for her. She should never have married me."

Sir Geoffrey searched his mind for a proper response for quite a long time before he understood that none was needed, and indeed that his proud cousin would have taken severe offense if such was suggested.

"It looks bad, Geoff. Damned bad! In fact, it seems that we have become the scandal of London! Did m'grandmother tell you that Cassie's indiscretion in Covent Garden had reached even her ears? She summoned us here under false pretenses, tellin' us she was on her deathbed. And we arrive only to find that she's makin' plans for some damned party or other! Lord, I wish I had never agreed to this marriage, for it's led me into a tangle! I was a blind fool to believe that Cassie and I should be able to deal along! I'm a quiet man, I dislike trottin' all over the town. When I saw her up on the box with Ardmore in the park th'other day, it was outside of enough! But that night at Covent Garden was the final straw, particularly since I was givin' the other lady her farewell supper. I haven't seen her since!"

From this tortured utterance, Sir Geoffrey discerned that his cousin found no release in unburdening himself. "Oh, we parted all right and tight, with no hard feelings on either side, y'know! Seems she found a new baron who's got more of the ready to hand than I, if you can believe that. She's already makin' her plans to slip over to France with him, away from his wife! All long, Liza was playing me for what she could get, I'm beginning to think. The damned thing of it is, I really wanted to do the right thing by Cassie, but every time we go after it, we end up at loggerheads! She's always in and out of one of her damned scrapes. Perhaps it would have been better for her to have met Ardmore first! I—I feel very deeply for Cassie. Well, can't know a female since she was in leading strings and not feel something for her, y'know. With the right sort of clothes and all, she's actually a rather fetching little thing. No great beauty, of course, but something to think about." He stared into the murky red wine morosely. "It was supposed to be a marriage of convenience, no attachments on either side, but how was I to know that she'd cut a dash in Society? I ought to cut her loose, allow her to take her head. If I went abroad for a while, she would have the freedom she needs to choose the right man for herself. You'd keep an eye on her. But I'm not the right man. I can't cut a leg or pay her address, or sit through those damned plays and operas that she likes so much. No, Geoff, I must let her go. It's not her fault. It's mine, for I have been a wretch!"

After a long interval of silence, during which the port was dropping at a steady level, Sir Geoffrey gently suggested that they join the ladies.

Unhappily, this suggestion did not fare well. Cassandra, pleading a headache, had refused to play piquet with the Dowager. Julia, drafted in her stead, was inept, and causing the Dowager no end of frustration in her attempts to instruct Julia in the rules of the game.

" 'Pon rep, child! That is the third time you've trumped your own ace!" the Dowager exclaimed pettishly as the two gentlemen entered the scene.

Julia, clearly bored, tossed her cards down on the table. "Oh, I don't care! Piquet is a dull game anyway, and Geoffrey plays much better than I do, as well you know, Grand'mère!"

Cassandra began to scrape the cards up from the table, while the Dowager muttered about ungrateful children. "Geoff! Come and play, and you too, Edward! We shall make up one or two sets and then I shall retire to bed. It has been a long day, and tomorrow will be worse!"

Julia walked over and sat down at the piano, where she began to grind out a rather badly played sonata.

With a sigh, Edward and Sir Geoffrey sat down at the table. Cassandra awkwardly shuffled the cards and dealt them each a round hand. The play commenced in rather a dull fashion, with the Dowager bidding three high hearts, and Edward trumping her with spades.

Sir Geoffrey played automatically, wishing himself elsewhere. He was an adequate player, but the lack of stakes bored him, and the Dowager's mood seemed to be matched by Edward's; even without stakes, they were both cut-throat players who loved to win.

The play continued on, however, for what seemed like hours before Cassandra, also a rather timid player when faced with the Dowager and Edward at table, made the foolish mistake of bidding against her own hand.

"Must you be stupid, on top of everything else?" Edward demanded impatiently, throwing in his cards. He had spoken impulsively, and without thinking, but Cassandra paled and recoiled as if he had slapped her. Without a word she lay down her hand and left the room, ignoring both his apologies and the other players begging her to return to the game.

The hallway was dark, but a faint shaft of moonlight illuminated familiar objects. Without really thinking, Cassandra put out her hand to touch a heavy brass servière that stood in the corner. From the cold touch of that object, she was able to find her bearings, and proceeded into the library.

It was illuminated only by a shaft of silvery moonlight that fell across the hearthrug and touched with light the long line of a suit of armor. Through the open curtains, she could see the moon hanging just above the cove, touching the water with a thousand dancing diamonds, spreading long cool fingers of pale gray across the long lawn.

She felt her way across the room toward the couch, where she could sit and look out upon this scene and collect her thoughts.

Suddenly, the toe of her slipper touched something soft and solid that should not have been there. Cautiously, she drew back and looked down. A large, rather rumpled shape lay sprawled across the floor, only dimly visible in the half-light.

Puzzled, Cassandra picked up the flint and wheel from its place on the mantel and struck a light to the candelabrum there. Slowly the flame caught and rose on the air, and Cassandra picked up the branch to see what lay across the floor.

At first, she could not believe it. She stood stock still, looking down at the mass which had suddenly sprung into a shape far too real.

When she found her voice, after what seemed like hours, she tried to scream, but the only sound she could make was a faint moan. She could not remove her eyes from the sight on the floor, only standing stupidly, staring at it in mounting horror.

After what seemed to be forever, the library door opened.

Cassandra spun, dropping the candelabrum. It crashed to the floor, the flame guttering against the parquet before it died.

"Cassie, I just wanted to say that I was—"

Edward's voice, dear and familiar, filled her with relief. Without thinking, she ran to him, wrapping her arms about his neck, feeling his arms about her. "What's the matter, did I give you a fright? I didn't mean to."

It took Cassandra several seconds to find her voice, while she clung to Edward's dear, protectively warm embrace. When she was finally able to speak, she looked up at him. "Edward," she said in a small, choked voice. "Edward—it's—it's she! She's—she's dead!"

"What? Who?" Edward asked, puzzled.

Cassandra pressed her face into his chest. "It's Lady Chantry." She looked up at him, her face wild and pale in the moonlight. "And she's been strangled, Edward, strangled with my blue spangled scarf!"

CHAPTER 10

EDWARD laughed. It made a hollow sound in the still-closed room. He held Cassandra for a few moments, until he was certain that she was not about to faint, and then, placing her firmly on the sofa and advising her not to move, he picked up the candelabrum and lit all six lights, flooding the room.

When he looked down at the shape on the floor before the hearth, he did not have to see the face to know that it was Liza Chantry, in a lilac pelisse, lying in a crumpled heap, the spangled blue scarf drawn tightly about her neck.

Cassandra had begun to sob, drily and silently, more from shock than grief. She held herself, shivering and shaking her head from side to side.

Edward, who had seen many dead, knew what to do. He knelt over the body and picked up the wrist. It was pale beneath the hand beringed and gloved with lavender kid—already cold. But nonetheless he felt for the pulse. When he found there was none, he straightened up, frowning.

His eyes met Cassandra's. "Dead?" she asked.

Edward nodded briefly. "And I would guess that she's been dead for quite some time. But how—why? Here!" He frowned, as the implications began to hammer home. "Here! How did she get here, and why?"

"I don't know," Cassandra said.

"I might have known," Edward said, apropos of nothing. He sat down on the sofa beside Cassandra, stroking her hair. "Are you all right?" he asked tenderly.

She nodded, choking back the last of her sobs. "I shall be, in a moment. Edward, it was the most awful thing—in the dark—I almost tripped over her!" She shuddered, and realized that she had been shivering for several minutes. With a great deal of effort, she regained her composure, but she could not bring herself to look at Lady Chantry.

Both of them sat quietly for a moment, absorbing this unexpected development, trying to transfer their shock into reality.

"I don't know what she was doing here," Edward said at last.

"I just might."

They both turned to see Grubb standing in the doorway, bearing a lamp. Reflecting in the light, his face looked eerie as he nodded at them.

Edward was swiftly on his feet, his hand resting protectively on Cassandra's shoulder. "Perhaps you know more about this than you're willing to tell," Edward suggested to the butler.

Grubb advanced into the room, placing the lamp on the table. "I just might, Duke, I just might." He bent over the body, turning it over. Swiftly, he examined the corpse as if he had a great deal of experience in these matters. "A right clean job, that," he said thoughtfully. "Someone mashed 'er maw, pressed it right, no doubt about that. I haven't seen such a clean job since we hung Mad Jack Peyser back in Oh-Three. Course his lay was coping 'em with a bit o' rope, but this is as neat a bit o' work as I've seen in quite a while."

He straightened up. "Liza Goudge, old Goudge's gal. Knew she'd come to a bad end. Just didn't know when." Having pronounced this epitaph, he dusted off his hands, and eyed the duke. "Don't touch nothin'. Against the King's bench to destroy the evidence, don't you know. Ar, it was going to come to the nubbin' cheat one way or the other. She was a gamy un and no doubt o' that."

Edward shook his head. "Grubb—Josiah Grubb of Bow Street!"

He was rewarded with a sly smile and a faint nod. "Knew you was a downy one, Your Grace, for a toff, of course. I did cast you a hint, though, at dinner."

"The Turkish Wonder in the counterfeiting!" Edward turned this over in his mind.

Grubb made a noise of assent in his teeth. "Thought a man who boxed with Jackson would understand that. One of my successes, Your Grace."

"You sent the Wonder to be deported."

"Aye." Grubb shrugged. "And a tough nut he was, too, but we managed to run him down." Grubb walked across the floor, his scatting eyes missing no detail of the room. He stood at the window, fingering the latch between thumb and forefinger. "Now, as to Liza Goudge, Your Grace, or Lady Chantry, as she was to become, she was one I would 'ave liked to have seen on the Botany Bay channels. Bad blood in that family and no mistaking. 'Er brother was sent to the gallows for killin' 'is own wife over a stolen diamond taken off a merchant in Bond Street. Liza 'ere—" He jerked his head carelessly toward the corpse and spoke as if his mind were elsewhere occupied, still fingering the latch between thumb and forefinger. "All the morts was crying buckets to see 'andsome Jack Goudge swing at Tyburn, but 'is own sister never blinked an eye, though we 'ad reason to believe that she'd copped the swag to Holland—that is, she'd gotten hold o' the sparkler and had it sold and cut up afore 'er brother was cold in the chains." Grubb rubbed his fingers together, then gave the window a slight push. It swung outward on its hinges, sending a gust of cold wind across the floor, stirring at the curtains and rippling through the dead woman's hair. " 'Ere's how she made her way in."

Edward bit his lip. "Certainly Lady Chantry came from rather humble beginnings. She never made any secrets of her origins. But—"

"She stayed with 'em, Duke. 'Er pa was a fencing cove who led a merry dance in Bear Alley. Ar, 'e died under a cloud, that one, but 'e taught 'is children the tricks o' the trade, as you might say. But Liza 'ere wasn't interested in no dipped petticoats and pewter pocket watches. She wanted the grand things—and she 'ad the brains to get 'em. We'd reason to suspect that 'alf the stolen flashers—that's jewels to you, Your Grace, that passed in and out o' London went through 'er hands and into

Holland. Nowt more of the petty little coves for 'er, but all the while, she was a-laughing at the quality lookin' down their noses at 'er, whilst she rummed over their flashers."

"See here, you cannot possibly say that Lady Chantry was a burglar—" Edward put in, unbelieving.

Grubb shook his head, and his small, darting eyes twinkled as he scraped a bit of caked mud away from the parquet under his fingernail. Holding his hand out, he crossed to the body and looked at her lavender half-boots. "Ah, no! But I don't doubt that she would 'ave, if she could 'ave. No, at the end, she was workin' with one other. They 'ad what you might call a partnership. This 'ere cove would do the breaking and entering and the copping the sparklers—the heavy work, as you will, and our Liza 'ere would do the sellin', then they'd split the profits. I'll wager a monkey it was a lot more comfortable for 'er than 'er former lines of occupation, dealin' with every cove in town. This way there were just the two o' them to do the work, and right nice work it was, I imagine. In a year's time, there'd be a million pounds between 'em." He shook his head from side to side. "Aye, she come in over the lawns—the mud on 'er shoes does match the mud on the floor."

"But who is the other person, the burglar?" Cassandra asked. "And how did he come into here to murder Lady Chantry?"

Grubb threw her a shrewd look. " 'O's to say t'other cove did 'er in, Your Grace? Am I to understand this 'ere bit o' finery about the deceased's throat belongs to you?"

Cassandra winced as if she had been struck. Slowly, she looked down at Grubb, her eyes meeting his intense, inscrutable gaze. "It—it is my scarf, yes. But I didn't—"

Grubb held up one hand. "Nor for me to say yey or nay, Your Grace, not yet. Coroner's inquest 'as to say we've got a murder, and the magistrate 'as jurisdiction over mine 'ere. But if they return a murder verdict, then I would 'ave to say that you 'ad a motive. Liza Chantry was pipin' the tune of your 'usband's dance, as all the world knows, and you weren't too 'appy. And you've got a temper, as you might say."

Cassandra gasped, shaking her head. Her green eyes were very wide. "Oh, no—I couldn't—"

"I think we have had enough of this course, Grubb!" Edward said sharply, putting his hand on Cassandra's shoulder. "My wife is incapable of killing a fly, much less a human being! Your ideas are preposterous!"

Grubb straightened himself up, thrusting his hands deep into his pockets. He regarded Edward from beneath his eyebrows. "Females, Your Grace, is strange creatures, and deep! Particularly where there's a man involved!" He coughed. "Anyway, that's not to say that you couldn't have snuffed her spark either! Former ladybirds can be more tiresome alive than dead. You married m'lady 'ere, as all the world knows, because she was Golden Ball Russell's daughter, and as rich as could hold together. Now, if she was to be out of the way, in one fashion or another, such as bein' hung for killing your mistress, 'o'd come into the fortune? Kill two birds wi' one stone, as you might say."

"Do I understand you to say that I would set my wife

up for the murder of my former mistress to inherit her fortune?"

Grubb shrugged eloquently. "Not be the first time. Whatever, 'oever done it, it do look as if it were done in a right cool manner. 'Oever done it, 'e or she knew what they was about for the time."

"Well, what of this partner of hers? Is it possible that he could have trailed her down here and come upon her here somehow?" Edward demanded. "If, as you speculate, she had come to blackmail one of us, then he would surely know what she was about. Perhaps she had swindled him in the same fashion she swindled her brother."

Grubb nodded. "The diamond's not about 'er. You can see that for yourself. So that leaves us with yet a third suspect. 'Ave to see if there be anyone suspicious lurkin' about the neighbor'ood."

"If I were you, Grubb, I would set about it immediately, instead of accusing an innocent damsel of murder! By God, man, you stand here accusing my wife of murder when the culprit may already be long gone."

Unconsciously, his arm stole protectively about Cassandra's shaking shoulders, and their hands intertwined as they both looked up at Grubb.

The runner, however, remained unmoved. "And what's to say that you're not the partner what's been doin' the robberies all the while? A ton gent keeps himself in good shape, with a taste for adventure and a lean purse—and a close friendship with the lady in question 'ere—why, you'd know just 'ow to go about it, wouldn't you?"

"Never Edward!" Cassandra cried, rising from her chair. "You would never find a man with a higher sense of honor than my husband. Perhaps—perhaps things have not always been just as they should between us, but I have known him all my life, and the duke is *not* a thief or an adventurer. It is not at all in his way!"

"Calm yourself, Cassie," Edward soothed, drawing her close to himself protectively. He addressed Grubb with all of his ducal hauteur. "I have nothing to explain to you, Grubb. And neither does Her Grace. If necessary, I would be willing to swear that she has never left my side since we arrived at Woodland Manor!"

Cassandra raised her head. "And I should be willing to swear the same, upon my honor!" Her fingers dug into Edward's shoulder fiercely.

Grubb's eyes passed from one to the other, and he shrugged. "Be that as it may, what's to say the two of you ain't in it together?" he suggested.

"Grubb! I have been ringing for you the past half-hour. Whatever are you doing—" The Dowager brought herself up short in the doorway, looking down her nose at the body of Lady Chantry on the floor as if confronted with an unattractive insect. The color rose and drained from her face, but her expression did not change. "Well, really," she said at last. "What could one expect? Such a dreadful woman, a really trying female. It's a great deal too bad, Grubb, for I imagine she was more use to you alive than dead, but really I wish she would have chosen somewhere else to die."

The Dowager sank into a chair and snapped her fan for emphasis. "However, I daresay that now she has had the nerve to die in my home, we shall be forced to deal with it. I take it she met her death at the hands of our suspect?"

"Grand'mère! What do you know about this?" Edward demanded.

The Dowager's hands worked at the strings of her fan, betraying the strain under which she labored. "More, I fear, Edward, than I should really care to think about. Grubb was kind enough to allow me into his confidence from the start, when he first elicited my cooperation in this most sordid matter. Had I known then that it would lead us all into this tangle of murder—" She squared her shoulders and leveled her gaze at them, every inch the duchess. "I should have still seen my duty. But really, Edward," she added pettishly, "why you could not have formed a sensible attachment with some very dull opera dancer or an actress, like your grandfather did, instead of with a villainess and a criminal, I do not know. It has really been too bad of you. Jewel robbery and blackmail and smuggling stolen goods and heaven only knows what all! 'Pon rep, trying to blackmail *me* was outside of enough! Dreadful creature!"

"Blackmail you? Why should Liza want to blackmail you?" Edward demanded.

"Nothing *I* had done, I assure you!" the Dowager said evenly. She drew a level glance at Edward. "Lord knows, my sins have always been public enough to stand the strain. No, Edward, it was your sins she wanted to keep silent. In short, your relationship with her."

"E-Edward?" Cassandra's voice quavered. "But Edward has never done anything to—" Her hand closed around his, and she was unable to finish her sentence.

"Well, why want to keep quiet what all the world knows about? Foolishness, and so I told her, to her brazen face!" The Dowager sniffed. "I sent her packing with a strong set-down, I assure you! 'You may tell the world and be damned, madam,' I said to her, 'for I am certain you would do nothing to add to the world's knowledge. And furthermore, I have not a groat to give you, for the Woodlands, as you must know, have been blown to flinders for three generations.' Imagine her, giving herself the airs of a lady, when I could take one look at that dyed black hair of hers and tell you she was not!"

"But everyone knew about Edward and Lady Chantry! Why should she come to you and not to me?" Cassandra wondered. "She should have known that I would have given her anything to—" She broke off and looked down at her lap, unaware of the expression on her husband's face as he stared down at the top of her head.

He wondered if his hearing had betrayed him.

"So, you see, that was the point at which Grubb appeared. I must admit, at first I thought that he must be an accomplice of Lady Chantry's, for his appearance is not calculated to make one believe that he is on the side of the authorities. But he presented his credentials, and explained to me that he had been following Lady Chantry about, trying to gather evidence against her in the Ombersley theft."

" 'Mongst other things," Grubb said cheerfully as he threw an embroidered shawl over Lady Chantry's huddled form. "Bow Street's 'ad its eye on 'er for a long long time, tryin' to find enough evidence to arrest 'er and 'er partner together. 'Ate to see 'er go like that." He shook his head. "Almost gotten fond of 'er."

"Not precisely the sort of person one would wish to know," the Dowager put in. "But the accomplice, you see—"

"Beg pardon, Duchess, but that's all they need to know for the time bein'. But she was a-setting there at the Green Man in Woodland Green, just a-waiting for something, though I ain't sure what it might be—yet."

"And so, between the two of you, you've cast the net over my wife, myself, or both of us together! Well, a fine piece of work, but it won't do! I won't have Cassandra's name dragged through the mud, if I have to stand in the dock myself," Edward stated firmly.

Cassandra rose to her feet, crimson-flooded cheeks and green eyes flashing her protest. "No, Edward, I would see *myself* hanged before I'd let anyone hurt you!"

"Cassie! Mind yourself!" Edward said fiercely, putting his hand out to her.

"*Iffen* you will be good enough to cast your thought-box backward, Your Grace," Grubb said drily, "you will remember that I 'aven't said anything 'bout either o' you actually doin' the deed. I was just castin' out the line that might be taken, lessen we can find the other party—the partner—and tie this up all right and tight, as you might say. But wi'out evidence to the contrary, I'm proper boxed into a 'ole."

"Edward, Grubb will need all of our assistance if this murderer is to get justice," the Dowager put in. "Without our help, there could very well be trouble for all of us."

Edward turned away from Cassandra with one last speaking look. She took his hand in her own and held it very tightly. "I assure you, Grubb, you will have my fullest cooperation. But, you have given me very little to go on concerning the identity of Lady Chantry's partner."

Grubb shrugged. "The simple fact is, we don't know very much about 'im at all. 'Oever 'e is, 'e's managed to elude us very well, always stayin' in the background. We don't even know why 'e'd kill the cat what laid the eggs, kill Liza Chantry."

"Unless it was for the Star of Bombay, or perhaps to avoid some double-cross. But why here?"

"That's a question what 'e can answer," Grubb said laconically. "But I will lay you this. Neither you nor 'Er Grace 'ere 'ad to do wi' it. I've been watchin' you very close, Duke, 'an you ain't the man to go on the casement lay."

"Edward—Cassie—oh!" Lady Julia burst into the room, standing stock still, looking down at the body on the floor. Her eyes grew very wide, and she clutched at her grandmother's arm for support. "Oh—"

Grubb regarded her speculatively. "Lady Julia, do you know this 'ere woman?"

The girl shook her head, too shocked to speak, her face pale and drained.

"Do you recognize this 'ere scarf what's wrapped about 'er maw box, then?"

Julia looked quickly at the scarf and then away. "It—it was on Cassandra's dressing table."

"Julia, that is Lady Chantry. She has been murdered," the Dowager said firmly, leading the girl to a chair out of sight of the body. "You must tell Grubb everything you know, my dear. He is not a butler at all, but a runner from Bow Street. Lady Chantry was involved in some very terrible things, and somehow, she came here tonight and met her doom. Someone strangled her with Cassandra's scarf. It could look very much as if it was either Edward or Cassandra who committed the crime, Julia, so you must tell us exactly what you know about that scarf." The Dowager pressed Julia's hand in her own. "You know that I would not ask you to do this, Julia, if your brother's and Cassandra's lives did not depend upon it."

Julia's face drew shut, and she shook her head. "I don't know anything about it, Grand'mère. Oh, I feel as if I will faint!" she murmured weakly, putting her fingers against her forehead. "Oh, that terrible thing, lying on the floor—"

"She's going to be ill," Edward said. "Grand'mère, can you get her upstairs? We can talk about this later, in private."

Julia shook her head at him. "It's always me you blame," she said weakly, the hysteria under the edge of her voice. "It's always me, isn't it? No matter what happens, you always blame me—send me away to schools, treat me like an outcast—"

"Take her upstairs, please," Edward said sharply. "Ring for Strawbridge."

Julia shook her head. "No!" she hissed at him, her eyes narrowed, her back ridged out of the chair. She lifted her finger toward him. "No! I won't be blamed for this! Yes, I took the scarf!"

CHAPTER
11

"ALWAYS me!" she repeated over and over again. "As if you thought that I planned this thing, this affliction! I won't have it! Yes, I did it—I took Cassandra's scarf, and I don't know why! I don't! It was just there, and the next moment, I was downstairs, and it was in my reticule, and I was so ashamed that I thrust it down into the sofa cushions! There! There! Now you have the entire story! Are you happy, Edward? Are you satisfied! Oh, Cassandra, I'm sorry, I'm sorry! I didn't mean to take your scarf. It isn't as if I am a thief! Please, Cassandra, don't hate me!" Julia burst into tears and collapsed back into the chair, as limp as a rag doll, clutching frantically at Cassandra's hand.

Cassandra smoothed the girl's brow, murmuring soothing words into her ear. Over Julia's dark head, her eyes met Edward's for a brief second, and she flinched.

The duke's face was drawn and tight, and his whole body seemed to mirror his disgust as he turned away.

Obviously, he found his sister's confession and its attendant anxieties a spectacle unworthy of his sympathy, Cassandra thought, and even as her heart swung again against her husband's coldness and lack of feeling, it went out to the miserable girl sobbing beside her. Throwing Edward's back a stiff look, she wrapped her arms about Julia's shoulders.

"I say, what's the donnybrook here?" Sir Geoffrey demanded. "A man can't even have a quiet moment with a glass of brandy and a thought to his vernal wardrobing without havin' some sort of—God Almighty! Ain't that— is she—? I say, dashed bad ton!" He took in the scene with a jaundiced eye, but his hand trembled as he raised his quizzing glass to stare at the body of Lady Chantry lying on the floor. "How comes this all about? By God, don't tell me—"

"Ar, Sir Geoffrey, what you see is true enough," Grubb said grimly. "Lady Chantry's been murdered."

Sir Geoffrey's hands fluttered to his snowy cravat. "Dashed bad ton," he repeated again. "Have a bloody great lot of constables and magistrates and whatnot overrunning the place. Who did it? Anyone we know?"

"Suspicion seems pretty evenly divided," Edward said drily. "But upon the latest revelations of my sister, we may at least be reasonably sure it was not Cassie, in a fit of jealousy."

This remark was enough to set Lady Julia off again, into a series of wailing protests.

"Your Grace, I think it would be best of us to excuse Lady Julia afore the servants catch wind o' this," Grubb suggested in an undertone. "I 'ave my reasons for wantin' this quiet for the time, and a female waterin'-pot ain't likely to help the situation."

Sir Geoffrey, however, had the situation well in hand.

Striding across the floor, he delivered one reluctant slap at Julia's cheek. "Now see here, my girl," he said sternly. "A dead woman's nothing to be upset about, particularly if it's Lady Chantry. Like as not, before you stick your spoon into the wall, you'll have to deal with worse. Buck up, Jule. Geoff is here to see that nothing will happen to you!" With noble resignation, he allowed Julia to collapse on his coat, sprinkling tears across his immaculate lapels. "Always had some influence on the gel, don't you know," he murmured in an embarrassed voice to the Dowager, who was wringing her hands, helpless in the face of this latest crisis.

"I think we should take her upstairs," Cassandra suggested. "Perhaps if she were to lie down with a glass of brandy and a few drops of Grey's Tonic, she would feel more the thing. I fear she has been pressed well beyond the limit of a girl her age in this night's work."

Sir Geoffrey nodded, slipping his arm under Julia's shoulders. "I don't know what's goin' on, and what's more, I don't want to know. Only mean I'd be stuck down here givin' testimony for weeks on end. Come now, my girl, Geoff's here to help you up the stairs, and Cassie will see that you lie down with somethin' to make you feel more the thing. Be just like old times, when I'd come down from Cambridge to find you in a pet over a broken doll or a sick cat. Up, Julia! That's a fine gel!"

She sniffled but did not provide resistance as Cassandra and Geoffrey gently led her from the room.

"Ruined m' coat—" Sir Geoffrey's voice trailed off. "Edward, whatever happened, I do not want to know, mind you! Murder is not at all in my line!" He threw the words earnestly over his shoulder as he disappeared up the stairs.

Upon hearing the closing of her granddaughter's door, the Dowager sank down once again into her chair. Her countenance was pallid and her lips were pressed tightly together. "A fine night's work!" she said reproachfully to Grubb. "You promised that none of this would come to light!"

Edward turned from the window and looked down at the small, foxlike man. "I warn you, Bow Street or no Bow Street, if as much as one breath of my sister's affliction escapes from this room, I shall throttle you within an inch of your life. You cannot possibly understand what Hell her compulsion to steal the most unnecessary objects has caused her in her young life—what torments she has been through over an illness that the best doctors assure us has no cure! And yet, I would rather see myself placed on the scandal block as a murderer than allow one word of it to destroy her reputation!"

Grubb nodded. "The Dowager 'as already threatened me with worse than yours, Duke! But I ain't about to send the little lady up on a pike! She don't concern us 'ere. What she says only makes the noose draw tighter about Liza Chantry's partner. Do y'see? It was 'e 'o found the scarf down and behind the sofa cushions—a 'andy weapon, you might say."

Edward's jaw tightened. "We waste time! The magistrate must be summoned at once. I shall send my groom—"

"Oh, no, Your Grace! Sendin' for the magistrate could raise the merry 'ell at this point." Grubb's animal eyes narrowed. "Then you'd see just 'ow fast the 'ole misery tangle would be the food o' gossip through the West Country. No, Duke, I fancy, if we put our 'eads together, we can trap our villain in 'is own string afore the dawn! I'm out to 'ave a look at the garden path wi' a candle. Perhaps there's somethin' there that could lead us aright. Will you come wi' me, you bein' more knowin' o' these grounds than I?"

Edward hesitated only a moment before picking up a taper. He threw open the casement window. "After you, my good man," he said drily, resigned to anything this night would bring.

Grubb shook his head. "I'm thinkin' it would be best to arm ourselves. We're dealin' with a dangerous rogue, y'know."

The duke nodded. "I have a brace of pistols in my study. Hold and I'll fetch us down our arms."

He was no sooner gone from the room than the Dowager let out a long sigh. "Grubb, you promised that none of this night's work would come out!" the Dowager accused him.

Grubb pushed his hand down into an inner pocket of his livery. In the flickering light of the tapers, it seemed as though ice or liquid fire were spilling over his dark coat as his fingers turned toward the Dowager.

"The Star of Bombay!" she exclaimed. "I'd know Sophia Ombersley's necklace anywhere—but how?"

The runner smiled as he placed the necklace in the Dowager's hands, watching her turn the idol's eye stone over in her fingers. "I lifted it off the deceased quietlike, when I was makin' the search. It were in a secret pocket in her pelisse, you see."

"Seventeen smaller stones and the one large one," the

Dowager murmured. "This is the star necklace, I would swear upon it. But why did you keep still about it? And why did the murderer not find it upon her, if this was what he desired so much?"

Grubb's eyes narrowed. " 'E 'ad not the time, Duchess. And I kept still about it to set the trap to bait our man— or woman—back to the corpse. Iffen we find as much as a 'air out there, I'll willing eat me groats."

The Dowager's face grew troubled. "This is becoming far from a game, Grubb," she said with a shiver, handing the necklace back to him as if it were made of fire. She sagged in her chair. "I—I am afraid now. Not for myself, but for what we may find."

"And well should you be, my lady, for tonight's work won't be pleasant."

"Pistols," Edward said drily, handing one fine Manton to the runner. "Be careful that you don't shoot me in the dark, will you?" He closed his hand about the second pistol.

Grubb nodded thoughtfully.

It was close on to midnight, to judge by the number of times the old grandfather clock in the hall swung and struck its pendulum, when Cassandra emerged from Julia's room. Cassandra's hair had come unpinned from its elaborate coiffure, and her ivory dinner dress had a rent in the bodice.

She paused for a moment, leaning against the door-jamb, listening to the sounds that an ancient house makes. All the other doorways were dark, the doors firmly closed against the night. With a long sigh, she picked up the flickering taper from the hall stand and started toward her own room.

The sound of boots on the staircase affrighted her, and she felt the hot wax dripping over her fingers as she drew back into the shadows.

An exhausted Edward pulled himself up the stairs, his pistol thrust army-style into his belt. The search of the grounds had been long and fruitless, to judge by his weary expression.

When he saw his wife, his brows rose slightly. "What news of my sister? Is she resting now?" he asked, sinking down on the bench.

Cassandra nodded. "Yes. Grey's Drops sent her off, but not before I had some chance to talk with her about her problem. Edward, why did you not think to inform me earlier? Did you believe that I could not be trusted with the secret of Julia's nerves? By treating her as a family disgrace, you have only intensified the problem," Cassandra said stiffly, the faintest edge of anger and tiredness in her voice.

Edward threw his head back. The light hollowed out his cheekbones, giving his long face a skeletal appearance. "Now you must play doctor?"

Cassandra wrapped her arms about her shoulders, as to contain her anger. "Someone must! You, evidently, have done everything to give Julia the feeling she is a criminal when, in truth, it is your very coldness which reinforces her—her affliction! The best course of treatment for her would be some love and attention from the brother she idolizes!"

"What? Julia?" Edward asked. "She's always been so independent, so needing of nothing!"

"And so neglected! Since the death of your parents, you and Godmamma have done nothing but place her in one boarding school after another! I believe she relates stealing little objects with which she has no attachment to stealing affection!"

"And so, our family disgrace is another very good reason for you to be able to see your way clear to leaving me," Edward said heatedly. "Cassie, you don't know what a—a disgrace we have had brought upon us by Julia's unspeakable habit! But perhaps now that you have been informed, however inadvertently, it will serve to increase your disgust of the Talbots even further."

"There is only one Talbot in whom I find much to be disgusted with," Cassandra replied, her color heightening.

"I imagine so. It cannot, after all, be such a very pleasant experience for you to find that there are certain things money cannot buy. Such as not being accused of murder."

"So, we've come back to that, have we?" Cassandra pressed thumb and forefinger against the bridge of her nose, shook her head, and suddenly stood up straight, glaring down at Edward. "And whose fault was that, pray tell? Who formed the acquaintance of that dreadful woman?"

"Touché, madam wife!" Edward laid his hand upon his knee, palm down. "But you will be pleased to know that as of yet, our entire sordid tale has not been dragged before the magistrates."

"Small wonder and greater pity! Why should the West Country not know that the Duke of Woodland suspects his wife of murdering his mistress?"

"Or vice versa?" His hand stole about her wrist, holding her tight as his eyes bored into her own. "I believe that you think me capable of murder, Cassandra!"

She shook her head violently. "No, no, I do not think that. Not always. You are capable of many things, Edward, but I wonder if murder is among them."

"Good Lord, Cassie!" He breathed, dragging her to her knees before him, her wrist held tightly in his grip. "What a night this has been! By God, if I were to murder anyone, my girl, it would surely be you!"

She wrested herself away from him, pale with fury. Without a word, she turned and ran down the hall.

CHAPTER
12

A silver pool of moonlight spilled across the carpet. The hallway was still, filled with the ticking of the grandfather clock on the landing. It whirred and struck twice, then was steadily ticking again.

A mouse scurried through the rotting wainscotting, leaving a trail of dusty footprints in its wake.

The thinnest sliver of light was visible from beneath Cassandra's door.

The Duchess of Woodland looked like nothing more than a frightened schoolgirl whose heart has been taxed beyond its powers. She sat motionless in the chair by the window, staring out across the lawn with unseeing eyes that were hollow and red-rimmed from weeping. Sleep, which might have eased her aching heart, would not come without nightmares of Edward's accusing face.

Suppose, just suppose, she thought, that Edward were the murderer and the burglar. It would explain much of his conduct. She shook her head from side to side, to clear this thought away. But again and again, it would come unbidden to her. If it were true, she would never betray him by the slightest word or gesture, no matter what. If he wished to rid himself of her, he would divorce her. But she would far rather he killed her, for life without him would be intolerable. . . .

A tear coursed slowly down her cheek, and she sighed aloud. It would be preferable to be as dead as Lady Chantry than to be cast aside by the only man she loved. Lord, there never was such a miserable tangle.

Unable to tolerate the torture of her own thoughts any longer, Cassandra rose and pressed her face against the cool glass panes of the window. It felt good against her fevered cheek.

Suddenly, she drew away from the window, then, breathless, looked down into the lawns again, along the garden path which led into the library. Cassandra, who had been brought up to distrust implicitly her own perceptions of life when compared to those of her elders, blinked again and again, as if she were seeing a mirage.

In the moonlight, almost as bright as day, the tiny

object glittered in the boxwoods, tantalizingly out of her line of vision. Crane as she might, Cassandra could not quite focus on it. It appeared to be a small white square, but what it could be she had no idea, for it seemed to have been dropped carelessly into the bushes along the path, too far away to be recognized.

Suddenly, it came upon her that this might be some clue that would implicate Edward in the murder. A coldness stole through her body as she contemplated its possible discovery by Grubb or the magistrates who would arrive in the morning.

"It must not be!" she told herself, and without a wasted thought, she picked up her dark traveling pelisse and threw it over her stained dinner gown.

It was the matter of a few seconds to steal into the hallway and down the stairs, feeling her way through the familiar house in darkness.

At the door of the library, she hesitated, thinking about the dead thing within, then turned and moved swiftly into the dining room, where another set of doors also gave way to the lawns and the terraces, sloping down to the sea.

The thought of saving Edward gave her courage to step into the outside world, where all that was dear and familiar might be another planet, so alien had it all become under the pale and deathlike light of the huge round moon that hung above the sea.

Ocean wind, cold and cutting, whipped about her face as she took a deep breath and stepped outside. The breakers, crashing against the rocks below the cliffs, sounded very near and very relentless.

But Cassandra was not the girl who had frighted the governess with bogles dressed in sheets, nor the perpetrator of a hundred other scrapes, to allow her courage to fail now. She stood quietly on the stone terrace, allowing her eyes to adjust to the darkness. With a deep breath, she stepped into the wet grass and moved toward the dark shapes of the boxwoods where she had seen the small white object.

Wind rustled through the ancient shrubbery. A more fanciful person might have ascribed this to ghosts or spirits or smugglers. But Cassandra's imagination was not poetic, and she thrust her arm into the bushes with determination. Her fingers closed upon a cold, hard square, and she allowed herself a grim smile of satisfaction.

The object in her hand was not nearly so grim or so mysterious as she might have wished it to be, had she read more of the Gothic novels so much in fashion. But it was puzzlingly familiar. A porcelain snuffbox, done all over with nymphs and cupids.

Cassandra turned it over in the palm of her hand, trying to recollect where she had seen it before. Much depended upon her memory now. . . .

It was as if she felt the noose tightening about Edward's neck. She closed her eyes and saw, in her mind's memory—

"Covent Garden!" The sound of her own voice startled her, and the memory of that odious night was still fresh enough to make her blush furiously. "Good God, Covent Garden!" she repeated in a lower voice, glancing over her shoulder at the quiet house. But nothing stirred, and her voice was whipped away by the wind. Again, she saw the box placed upon the table, and Liza Chantry's mocking face, challenging Cassandra to her own husband.

But Edward did not dip snuff, preferring his long cigarillos from Spain. He was innocent! Cassandra clutched the box to her breast, sending up a quiet prayer of thanksgiving.

"Cassie! What the deuce!"

Cassandra suppressed a shriek and spun around in her tracks. Her heart was in her throat. And then, quite as soon as her terror had come, it abated. "Oh, Geoff! It is only you!" she said accusingly as Sir Geoffrey Russell-Broome emerged from the shadows, immaculate as usual in a dark cloak. The whiteness of his neckcloth and cravat seemed to glow faintly in the half-light. "Indeed, I might ask you the same question, cousin!"

Sir Geoffrey shrugged. "Couldn't sleep. Dash it, girl, veal on top of murder don't sit well, you should know that! Took a stroll to clear out my head." He approached her slowly.

"I—I couldn't sleep either, so I took a walk." Cassandra said lamely, clutching the snuffbox in her hand. A cold prickling stole along her neck as she suddenly remembered to whom that snuffbox had belonged. Her heart thundered in her ears, and she hoped that he could not sense her growing terror.

"Dashed bad ton to be wanderin' about the lawns at night, Cassie. Make people think you're as mad as one of those Cheltenham heroines, Cass!"

His voice was so reassuringly Geoffrey, the cousin she had known and trusted and loved all her life, that Cassandra had a moment of doubt. It could not be possible, she thought, not Geoff, not dear, foppish Geoff. And yet—

There was a vague, threatening coldness in his eyes as he approached her, a certain sinuous strength in his movement that she had never noticed before. It took every ounce of her courage not to turn and run, but to allow him to stand right by her. "I say, Cassie, what's that I saw you fishin' out of the boxwoods?" he asked.

Cassandra laughed. It sounded hollow in her own ears. "Oh, just a bracelet. I—I was leaning over the balcony, looking at the moon, and the catch opened, and the bracelet fell into the shrubbery—Geoff!"

He had seized her wrist in a steel grip, forcing her fingers to open, dropping the snuffbox into his palm. His grip on her did not release as he examined the snuffbox in a leisurely fashion. It was then that she was certain of it, and torn between grief and shock. Dear, imperturbable, faithful Geoff—leading a double life as a thief and a murderer. The shock was so great that she could only stand and peer into his face, as if begging him to deny this moon-folly, to be her dear, beloved cousin again, abjuring her to run inside and be a good girl, before she spoiled her slippers.

But Sir Geoffrey lifted his lip in a slight sneer and met her eyes with a look of such undisguised contempt that she gasped in hurt and anger—and fear.

"Always too smart for your good, Cassie, always into one of your scrapes and askin' dear cousin to rescue you." He shook his head. "I warned you, Cassie, against such scrapes, don't you know. But now, I fear it's too late for you. This is one scrape I cannot protect you from, my girl." His voice was as lazy, as drawling as ever, without a hint of the fear and anger he must be feeling.

Cassandra was too numb to struggle. She could only watch his face, searching for the sinister implications of his character. "Not you. Not you, Geoff," she heard herself saying accusingly.

Sir Geoffrey lifted one shoulder in an elegant shrug. "Always too trustin', Cassie, too trustin' by half, my girl. Told your aunt you should have been put upon the world a bit before your come-out, but her plans were otherwise." He shook his head sorrowfully. "All would have been right, don't you know, if Edward had died in the wars, or if you had come to me with your marriage proposal. For I believe you would have, don't you know, if he hadn't come strollin' about to your come-out party." She felt his fingers digging into her wrist. "Then you would have married me, and the fortune would have come to me all right and tight. I would have been able to end my double life much sooner, retirin' as a gentleman. Could have paid poor greedy Liza off, and she'd still be alive. Lord, she did love life." He shook his head, and Cassandra listened in fascinated horror, barely comprehending his words. "But you married Edward, and she was too greedy by half. So I had to dispose of her. God, how she hated you. You had youth and fortune . . . and Edward. That was too much for her. She would have done anything to push you out of the way. Made the mistake of fallin' in love with him, foolish woman. She meant to tell him all, hoping to get your money out of him in return for his silence. Edward would never betray the family, after all." Sir Geoffrey shook his head. "See how long he protected Julia! He would have offered me a goodly sum to take myself off to Europe, live on the Continent, away from English law. But, dash it, I'm not a man to run. Not from the damned English law, when I've outrun them all. Easiest thing in the world to befriend a woman and bring her into fashion. Easiest way to find out how and where she keeps her baubles. And then, when the time's right—steal 'em."

The wind rustled around his words. His voice was almost dreamlike, as if he enjoyed revealing his triumphs to his little cousin. "For a man with a taste for the boodle, and a position in Society, but no money, it's a dashed hard life, Cassie. M'father didn't leave me a feather to fly with. I had to do something. Never meant it to come to murder—bad ton, murder—but stands to reason. With Liza out of the way, I'll come into your fortune *and* the title at one swoop."

"But—but—" Cassandra heard her teeth chattering. She attempted to work her hand out of Sir Geoffrey's grip, but he only increased his hold, looking dreamily over her head.

"Simply, my dear Cassie, by doin' nothin', and allowing the law to take its course. Edward, after all, was known to be a good friend of Liza's. What would make more sense than his becomin' the thief and the murderer? Known to be done up for years with an expensive mistress. Mistress gets tiresome, the wife he married for her fortune is even more tiresome. Why, who would think that dear old Geoffrey would murder anyone? Edward will be the man they'll hang for the crimes, and I shall be sympathetic, but a most excellent witness for the defense, don't you know? And with both of you out of the way, I shall have both fortune and title. Daresay I would make a better duke than Edward. More of a sense of what's due me. And I've worked for it, of course."

Cassandra shivered, unable to move, as his inexorable voice fit together the pieces of the puzzle. Even she had suspected Edward! Those who had little reason to hold him in affection would be swifter to point an accusing finger at him. And who in all the world would ever, even in jest, suspect vain, foppish Sir Geoffrey Russell-Broome?

"I really didn't want this to happen, Cassie. I hope you understand, my girl," Sir Geoffrey said softly. "But some things are inevitable, don't you know. It was a great deal too bad that you had to see that snuffbox in the bushes. Dropped it there when I was leadin' Liza into the library for what she thought would be an interview with Edward! Poor wretch—love blinded her good sense! If you had only allowed me to fetch it back myself, Cassie, you would have come 'round and married me. But this circumvents that action. Never was a marryin' man anyway."

Cassandra saw her chance and desperately took it. With a sudden movement, she twisted her arm in Geoffrey's grip and started to run.

It was the worst thing she could have done, for he was larger and stronger than she, and quickly had seized her around the waist. In her panic, she felt his fingers pressing to her throat, and her own gasping struggles for breath were as useless as a leaf against the wind. The edges of her consciousness were black, and the blackness was seeping over her panic into a sort of terrible resignation. She wanted to scream, but there was nothing there but a sense of helplessness and despair. Edward was the only thing in her mind. If she must die, she would hold his image as the last thought she had on earth.

From a far distance away, she thought she heard shouting, thought that she felt the blessed release, that she was gulping great mouthfuls of air.

"Stop! Duke, stop!" she thought she heard Grubb saying. "Let 'im 'ang for 'is crimes!"

Then there were strong hands on her shoulders, hands holding her away from the blackness. She heard her own voice dimly croaking, "Not Geoff, oh, not Geoff!"

And somewhere, very close by there was the feel of a familiar shoulder and a dear voice whispering into her ear the words she never thought she would hear. "Cassie, oh, Lord, Cassie, if I had lost you, I would have lost all reason for living—"

"Edward—" Cassie choked, and for the first time in her life, fainted.

CHAPTER
13

THE first strains of the country dance floated up the stairs from the ballroom. Voices and laughter were heard below in the hall as the first dinner guests made their arrival.

"Well, Augusta. And quite a time you've had of it of

late!" Sir John Rawdon's booming laugh was followed by a reassuring Georgian chuckle from the Dowager.

"La, Jack, quite an adventure, I assure you! Do come in and allow me to tell you all about it."

Lady Julia's dark head floated in the mirror above her sister-in-law's straw-colored curls. There was a certain new understanding in both pairs of eyes as they met in the glass. Julia smiled. "There, my love. Grand'mère was quite right about the cucumber poultice. The bruises are barely visible now. And a bit of lace about your throat makes you look the more interesting. Do you feel well enough to come down to dinner? After all, this is your first day out of bed, and you know what the doctor said—"

Cassandra gave her sister-in-law's hand a reassuring squeeze. "In truth, Julia, I look far worse than I feel." She bit her lip, and touched the hollows of her cheeks.

"And perhaps you would feel much better if Edward had come to see you at least once while you were down," Julia said wisely. "He's been so distant and aloof from us all that I wonder what is in his mind. But he did the most extraordinary thing this morning. He proposed to me that he and I should have more time together. He asked me if I would like to learn to handle the reins of his phaeton, which, of course, I should like above all things, for Edward is a credible whip! And then he said that perhaps it was time that he had shown me some proof of his affection and concern for me in a positive manner, rather than taking me down a peg every time I opened my mouth! I was quite pleased." Her fingers flew deftly over

Cassandra's curls. "There! I think it was a very good thing that Lavinia and I spent so much time doing up one another's hair at school, for I think I have managed to turn you out quite credibly! And, Cassandra, Edward says I need not go back to school, that I may live with Grand'mère and have a tutor until it is time for my come-out!"

Cassandra forced herself to smile. "I am so glad for you and Edward, Julia," she said sincerely. "It is good that brothers and sisters be close. I never had a brother or a sister—before!" She again squeezed Julia's hand for emphasis and gave her a sweet, sad smile.

Julia impulsively hugged her. "But if it were not for you, Cassie—oh, I have no words to express it! But you know that we—I and Grand'mère, at least—love you and care about you!"

Cassandra nodded, unable to speak. She held her sister-in-law at arm's length, admiring the pretty ball dress of sprigged silk, in contrast to her own more sophisticated gown of palest green sarsnet with silver embroidery. "I hope you shall always be happy," Cassandra told Julia.

"And I hope that you shall find happiness," Julia replied, "whatever happens. Oh, Grand'mère is calling me to come down and make my bow to the guests. She says I may have two country dances, for I must learn how to go about in company before I am at Almack's. Dearest Cassie—"

Another impulsive hug and she was gone.

More slowly, Cassandra rose from the dressing table. She pulled the tiny bit of lace up over the dark discolorations on her throat, closing her eyes as she remembered the horrors of that night.

She turned from the mirror and picked up her little satin reticule from the chair, determined to face the guests with grace, if not with style. If only he had come to her in her illness. If only he—

There was a quiet knock at the door, and Edward slid quietly into the room, tall and imposing in his black evening dress. He too, showed traces of the past few days' events in his hollow eyes and sad expression.

In the candlelight, Cassandra thought she saw the first streaks of gray in his hair.

They looked at one another for a long moment, without moving. Each one seemed to withdraw into an invisible protection of armor.

Cassandra picked up her shawl. "Do you come to give me escort to dinner, husband?" she asked in an unnaturally gay voice. "After being upon my bed for so long, I feel the need to be in company again. Perhaps, for propriety's sake, you will spare at least one dance for your wife."

"Cassandra," Edward said slowly. There was something in his voice that forced her to look up at him. He stood before her stripped of his cold and cynical demeanor, as much like a young man as he had been before he had gone to war. "Cassandra, I can wait no longer. I have come to ask for your decision."

"Decision? What decision, Edward?" she asked, genuinely puzzled. Edward paced about the room, unable to look at her. "I believed it best to wait until you were fully recovered to ask you, lest I take advantage of your innocence yet another time." He turned to face her, his eyes expressionless on the surface, yet beneath their cold grayness, betraying a mixture of emotions. "I have been a bad bargain from the start, Cassandra. A stiff-necked, prideful, selfish wretch, so caught up in my own beliefs that I should never feel any tender emotion again that I have taken advantage of you at every turn."

Cassandra shook her head. "Oh, no, Edward, it has been I, leading you into this mad scheme of marriage, entering into every folly of the Town that crossed my path, interfering in your life when I did not mean to. I have not been a good wife, Edward!"

"The time for recriminations is past, Cassie. I have done more harm to you than I ever dreamed possible, dragging your name through these scandals. I—"

"Geoffrey is my cousin also," Cassandra said sadly. "If only I had known how desperately he needed money—it never meant that much to me to be as rich as a nabob. I—I would have been happy if I had nothing. Then all this would never have come to pass."

Edward nodded. "And I, I would have been happier to never have been born a duke! Then perhaps I might have seen you for what you are, for what I feel for you." He squared his shoulders. "I have come to tell you that if you should wish to file for divorce, or should wish me to leave the country to spare you further pain, I would do so."

"Oh, no Edward!" Cassandra cried. Impulsively, she reached out to him. "If you—you feel for me at all, please do not speak in such a way! For if I could not at least see you, I—I think I should pine away and die! I cannot hold it any longer, Edward. I must tell you the truth. And then you must decide what to do with me. I told you before that I had felt only a schoolgirl's tendre for you—frivolous and fleeting as the wind. But I have been truly and deeply in love with you ever since I was old enough to understand what the word meant! Only the situation at Aunt Gunneston's would have forced me to come to you for—for help, though. It was a mad and foolish thing to do, for it could only cause pain—for I know that you do not love me."

"Do not love you?" Edward asked incredulously. "But —well, it's a dashed bad thing when a man has wanted to kiss his own wife anytime these past months, and take her in his arms and tell her he loves her, with only his damned pride preventing him."

He suited his actions to his words with such vehemence that Cassandra found her breath taken away as his lips crushed against her own and she was held very tightly in his arms. She did not mind in the least that he was disarranging her hair, or that the dinner guests were patiently awaiting them below. Instead, she threw her arms about his shoulders and clung to him for dear life, as if afraid that this moment would melt.

"There is only one thing, if you please, Edward," she said meekly when he allowed her to catch her breath.

"What is that, my love?" he asked, his breath light against her ear.

"If you would please, for once, just say you love me— I would not ask for anything else."

Edward laughed, looking down into her green eyes. Gently, he stroked her straw-colored curls. "Lady Cassandra Russell, I love you with all of my heart! And so I shall prove to you!"

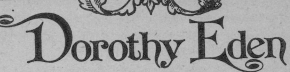

Dorothy Eden

*One of today's outstanding novelists writes tales about
love, intrigue, wealth, power—and, of course, romance.
Here are romantic novels of suspense at their best.*

Phyllis A. Whitney

*Beautifully written stories of love, intrigue and mystery
put together as only Phyllis Whitney can.*

☐ BLACK AMBER	23943-8	$1.95
☐ BLUE FIRE	23537-8	$1.50
☐ COLUMBELLA	22919-X	$1.75
☐ EVER AFTER	23425-8	$1.75
☐ THE GOLDEN UNICORN	23104-6	$1.95
☐ HUNTER'S GREEN	23523-8	$1.95
☐ LISTEN FOR THE WHISPERER	23156-9	$1.75
☐ LOST ISLAND	23886-5	$1.95
☐ THE MOONFLOWER	23626-9	$1.75
☐ THE QUICKSILVER POOL	23983-7	$1.95
☐ SEA JADE	23501-7	$1.75
☐ SEVEN TEARS FOR APOLLO	23428-2	$1.75
☐ SILVERHILL	23592-0	$1.75
☐ SKYE CAMERON	23403-7	$1.75
☐ SNOWFIRE	23628-5	$1.75
☐ SPINDRIFT	22746-4	$1.95
☐ THUNDER HEIGHTS	24143-2	$1.95
☐ THE TREMBLING HILLS	23539-4	$1.95
☐ THE TURQUOISE MASK	23470-1	$1.95
☐ WINDOW ON THE SQUARE	23627-7	$1.75
☐ THE WINTER PEOPLE	23681-1	$1.75

Historical Romance

Sparkling novels of love and conquest against the colorful background of historical England. Here are books you will savor word by word, page by spellbinding page.

☐ TRUMPET FOR A WALLED CITY—Pala	23913-6	$1.75
☐ THE ARDENT SUITOR—Greenlea	23914-4	$1.75
☐ HONEY-POT—Stables	23915-2	$1.75
☐ SOPHIA AND AUGUSTA—Clark	23916-0	$1.75
☐ THE WITCH FROM THE SEA—Carr	22837-1	$1.95
☐ AFTER THE STORM—Williams	23928-4	$1.75
☐ ALTHEA—Robins	23268-9	$1.50
☐ AMETHYST LOVE—Danton	23400-2	$1.50
☐ AN AFFAIR OF THE HEART Smith	23092-9	$1.50
☐ AUNT SOPHIE'S DIAMONDS Smith	23378-2	$1.50
☐ A BANBURY TALE—MacKeever	23174-7	$1.50
☐ CLARISSA—Arnett	22893-2	$1.50
☐ DEVIL'S BRIDE—Edwards	23176-3	$1.50
☐ ESCAPADE—Smith	23232-8	$1.50
☐ A FAMILY AFFAIR—Mellow	22967-X	$1.50
☐ THE FORTUNE SEEKER Greenlea	23301-4	$1.50
☐ THE FINE AND HANDSOME CAPTAIN—Lynch	23269-7	$1.50
☐ FIRE OPALS—Danton	23984-5	$1.75

Buy them at your local bookstores or use this handy coupon for ordering: